A Most Inconvenient Earl

The Brides of North Barrows #4

CLAIRE DELACROIX

Books by Claire Delacroix

MEDIEVAL ROMANCE

Blood Brothers
The Wolf & the Witch
The Hunter & the Heiress

The Champions of St. Euphemia
The Crusader's Bride
The Crusader's Heart
The Crusader's Kiss
The Crusader's Vow
The Crusader's Handfast

The Rogues of Ravensmuir:
The Rogue
The Scoundrel
The Warrior

The Jewels of Kinfairlie:
The Beauty Bride
The Rose Red Bride
The Snow White Bride
The Ballad of Rosamunde

The True Love Brides:
The Renegade's Heart
The Highlander's Curse
The Frost Maiden's Kiss
The Warrior's Prize

The Brides of Inverfyre:
The Mercenary's Bride
The Runaway Bride

Rogues & Angels:
One Knight Enchanted
One Knight's Return

The Bride Quest:
The Princess
The Damsel
The Heiress
The Countess
The Beauty
The Temptress

REGENCY ROMANCE

The Brides of North Barrows:
Something Wicked This Way Comes
A Duke by Any Other Name
A Baron for All Seasons
A Most Inconvenient Earl

TIME TRAVEL ROMANCE

Once Upon a Kiss
The Last Highlander
The Moonstone
Love Potion #9

For information about Deborah Cooke contemporary
romances and paranormal romances, please visit:

HTTP://DEBORAHCOOKE.COM

PROLOGUE

North Barrows, Cumbria—August 1815

Eurydice Goodenham stood with her hands folded before herself, watching as dirt struck the coffin.

Her grandmother, Octavia Hambley, Viscountess North Barrows, was dead. She had taken a chill in the spring and been unable to shake it. No matter which physician was summoned, the illness had persisted, lodging in her lungs with a tenacity that echoed the lady's own. Four months they had battled, illness and dowager, and in the end, the illness had won.

Eurydice could not help but feel she had overlooked some detail that might have ensured her grandmother's recovery. She had consulted every reference and made many suggestions, though none had helped. All said, she had done her best and more, but she was keenly aware that her best had been insufficient.

It was a hot day with a haze on the hills that promised at least a heavy dew that night, if not more. Eurydice was warm, even in her lightest summer muslin, but discomfort was irrelevant. She could not believe that her grandmother was dead, even though she had been granted custody of the dowager's beloved umbrella. She clutched it now, unwilling to relinquish it. It seemed fitting that the umbrella should attend the service, just as Nelson and the other servants did.

It was not the first time she had attended a funeral of someone she held close, but this time, Eurydice understood the ramifications of death better. Her parents had died when Eurydice had been only five, leaving her and her older sister alone. She remembered uncertainty but had never guessed at Daphne's terror of the future until told of it years later. She certainly remembered their grandmother arriving from Bath, austere and commanding, then sweeping them up on her way back to the North Barrows dower house. Lady Octavia had been stern but she had loved them fiercely and done her best for them.

Eurydice did recall her grandmother's relief when Daphne had wed the Duke of Inverfyre. He was a good man, kind to her sister and their children. Eurydice liked watching him with their two sons, Malcolm and Edmond. It was a revelation to her that a somber and sensible man could be so playful—even silly—with Malcolm the toddler, and the sight made her smile. She'd learned from his lullabies to the infant Edmond that he had a fine voice. He had been generous with their grandmother, as well, inviting her to stay whenever she chose, for as long as she chose. The duke had promised the viscountess that Eurydice was secure in his household for so long as she chose to remain, giving her the freedom to not wed at all. Eurydice knew he had brought Daphne from Airdfinnan near the end to repeat his vow to their grandmother one last time.

Lady Octavia had died convinced that her responsibilities were fulfilled.

The funeral for the viscountess was held at North Barrows, in the church where she had been married decades before, and she would be buried beside her beloved Alasdair, Viscount North Barrows. Upon the death of Eurydice and Daphne's father—Malcolm, the older son of Alasdair and Octavia—the estate had passed to his younger brother, Samuel, with the stipulation—made by Alasdair—that Octavia could reside in the dower house for her lifetime. The estate was currently held by Samuel's son and Eurydice's cousin, Daniel. He had permitted the party from Airdfinnan to stay at the dower house until the funeral and had even offered them whatever they desired of the furniture. Eurydice had no doubt that his wife had plans for the house, which was in need of renovation. She loved it as it was, but knew she was unlikely to ever cross its threshold again.

She gripped the umbrella, her throat tight as the dirt obscured the coffin. Daphne stood beside her, holding the duke's arm, their older son before them and the younger in the nursemaid's arms. Daniel and his wife and children stood on the opposite side of the grave. Nelson, the viscountess's lady's maid for years, sniffled loudly from the ranks of the servants. There were mourners gathered from the village, as well. The final blessing was pronounced and Eurydice let her tears fall.

Her life had been disrupted twice by death and left in uncertainty. It had been less of a shock this time, for her grandmother had faded visibly since Daphne's wedding, but still she was aware that her position was precarious.

The duke had given his word, but what if he died? What if he and Daphne were killed unexpectedly, as her own parents had been? All might go awry for Eurydice if her sister no longer drew breath. The children doubtless had a more secure future, the oldest being heir to the dukedom, but Eurydice felt that the ground was loose beneath her feet.

She had no desire to wed for romantic reasons, as Daphne had, but it made good sense to marry for practical ones. She would be able to guarantee her own future, then, if she chose wisely. Once she had made a jest that she would wed a rich rogue, but increasingly, she saw the merit of such a notion. The rake in question could continue to be a scoundrel in town, and she would retire to the country to read and write in peace.

It was a perfect scheme, for even if he died, she would inherit a measure of his wealth as his widow. In fact, she would ensure as much by making the provision in his will a stipulation of their match.

Fortunately, she knew a rogue who would suit her well.

All she needed was the audacity to propose to Sebastian Montgomery, Earl of Rockmorton—and the good fortune to have him accept.

CHAPTER ONE

Airdfinnan—November 1815

Sebastian Montgomery, Earl of Rockmorton, was enjoying a brandy in the library of his friend's Scottish house, Airdfinnan. It was a most suitable pastime for a day cursed with driving rain, though he consumed very little of the brandy. He swirled it in the glass and savored the scent of it, as was his custom.

He had received another letter from his mistress in London, the alluring Esmeralda Ballantyne, and truth be told, he did not wish to open it. He much preferred to watch the rain.

Doubtless the missive was filled with pledges of affection, requests for his return, paragraphs of yearning enough to make him yawn and ultimately, demands for some token of his supposed affections. Esmeralda had been different from other mistresses for years, but of late, she had become the same.

She had, despite her many charms, become predictable.

Sebastian despised this part of an affair. He had to break it off, but he also disliked being responsible for any woman's tears. Usually, he convinced himself that his mistresses' lamentations were contrived, and that all they truly loved was his generous spending.

He tired of flinging coin hither and yon. He tired of insincerity. He tired of fashionable society. And, to his own astonishment, he even tired of scandal.

Clearly, having his friends happily wed and merrily breeding was affecting his *bonhomie*.

He should have returned to London months before, but had lingered in Scotland all the same. He did not care to hunt particularly, though he did enjoy a bracing walk. What he liked was that his friend Alexander Armstrong's house was a home, for all its size and magnificence. He liked the open displays of affection between duke and duchess, the camaraderie between the servants and the unpredictability of two small boys, often bent on mischief. He had proven himself to be of assistance on such errands more than once.

Airdfinnan made him realize how solitary his own life had become.

Not that he had any plans to change his situation. Entanglements only led to disappointment, heartbreak and sorrow. No, Sebastian Montgomery had resolved twelve years before that his heart would never be shattered by loss again—and the sole way to achieve that objective, to his thinking, was to lead the life of a veritable hermit.

An occasional visit to Airdfinnan was simply a sample of the road not taken. It appealed precisely because it was so different from his own life, and he would not be seduced into making a terrible error.

Sebastian swirled the brandy and considered the wording of the missive he would send Esmeralda, terminating their arrangement. He would be polite but firm, as always he was. Resolute. If he did it by mail and immediately, by the time he returned to town, she would have found herself another lover. There would be no tedious scenes in public or awkward moments at the theater, and he would be able to seek a new recipient for his affections.

The other trouble was that he did not look forward to the search for a new nocturnal companion. He had always savored the hunt only when it came to women, but this particular chase had become so predictable.

What Sebastian desired most was a surprise. A challenge. A quest.

Even an adventure.

He was unlikely to find it in the duke's library in Scotland while the rain beat against the windows. Nor was he likely to discover it at the bottom of the brandy decanter. How tedious that at thirty-two, he suddenly had need of an occupation.

He was staring at the blank paper as if his letter would magically write itself when Miss Eurydice entered the library. She appeared to be unaware of his presence, but that did not surprise Sebastian. The younger sister of the duchess was often lost in her own thoughts or bent upon her own quests. She was definitely unlike other women of his acquaintance and, as a rare species of femininity, she interested him. It appeared that she sought a book in this particular moment, for she immediately began scanning the shelves.

It was a pity that she cared only for books. Since the marriage of the duke to her older sister, Daphne, several years before, Miss Eurydice had blossomed into a most enticing young woman. She had to be eighteen years of age by now and though Sebastian did not care in the least for maidens, he certainly admired the result. Her hair was still a darker blond than that of her sister, and she had grown taller, slimming through the waist and gaining more curves in a most attractive way. The view of her from behind was most charming. Sebastian could even glimpse her trim ankles when she stretched to reach a volume from a high shelf.

She had a general indifference about her appearance, which he liked. He disliked when women were concerned only with their hair or their faces—there was something more honest about Miss Eurydice's disregard for such details. This also meant that her hair was often in slight disarray despite her maid's herculean efforts. The curls that escaped their bonds fascinated Sebastian—there was nothing quite so feminine as a stray curl against a soft cheek, in his view, or anything more likely to tempt his touch. Such was the curse of unruly waves in her hair, he supposed, but the sight of her often reminded Sebastian of the look of a woman who had been thoroughly sampled. Had she been lounging abed with a satisfied smile, Miss Eurydice would have been a fine subject for a painting, one he could have looked upon for considerable time.

Perhaps that was why he noticed her, for Miss Eurydice had certainly not been sampled at all, much less thoroughly. Sebastian doubted her luscious lips, so faintly pink and full, had been kissed at all. The idea of changing that situation made him smile in the precise moment that she became aware that she was not alone.

His small sound of amusement—in imagining his friend Armstrong's outrage should he act upon his thoughts—might have been responsible for that change.

Miss Eurydice spun and glared at him, a becoming flush rising on her cheeks when she found him watching her. "You!" she said, with complete disregard for social convention. "Why do you always creep up on people?"

"I do not creep..."

"You most assuredly do, sir. This is not the first time I have found you watching me as if you meant to pounce." She marched toward him, apparently fearless, but hugged a book to her chest as if it might protect her. Her eyes narrowed, as if she wished to look dangerous. Sebastian thought she was delightful. "I would warn you not to have ideas, but I expect it is too late."

"Truly?"

"Truly. I believe you are the kind of man born with ideas."

Sebastian laughed. "Then you are a good judge of character, Miss Eurydice."

She looked back toward the door, then leaned closer, her expression intense. "Which is precisely why I would speak with you." Her voice was almost a whisper, so husky that Sebastian could not halt his sudden desire to touch her.

It was that cursed curl on her right cheek that was responsible.

Sebastian cleared his throat. "I beg your pardon?"

"I had hoped to find you alone."

Sebastian was surprised by this. It seemed to him that the last thing a respectable maiden should desire would be to find him alone.

"I would speak with you." She wrinkled her nose in a most delightful manner. "I would, in fact, request your assistance." As he watched, she perched on the desk, her manner confidential, and continued as if he had encouraged her. "I know you were of aid to Lady Anthea that winter in London and I find myself in need of similar...assistance." She met his gaze, her eyes bright with challenge.

They were hazel and thickly lashed, remarkably

lovely, in fact.

Sebastian straightened, fascinated. "Am I to know what manner of aid you need?"

"It is not complicated. Even you should be able to guess as much." She was still gripping the book as if her life depended upon it. He glanced down to see her ankle and calf revealed and in close proximity and felt a familiar heat surge through him. "You must have heard that they intend to give me a season." She rolled her eyes at the very prospect.

Sebastian grinned. "And you do not want one?"

"Of course, I do not want one! Why should I have any desire to attend parties and balls, to dance and to shop and to chatter with strangers?" This recitation of urban pleasures would have cast most young ladies of Sebastian's acquaintance into rhapsodies, but it was clear Miss Eurydice was not convinced. She shook her head in disgust and Sebastian fought his urge to smile.

That curl. She was adorable.

"It sounds abominable," he managed to say solemnly.

"It would be!"

"And what do you suggest instead?"

"I want to be left alone to read." She lowered her voice yet more. "Even *write*." She held his gaze for a long moment as if to assure him of her sincerity. "Why would I desire to go to London?" She didn't pause for him to reply. "But you know how the duke can be. He is certain it is the proper thing to do, and my sister is thrilled, and before I know it, I will be packed into the coach and headed south, condemned to *dancing*." This last she said with such scorn that Sebastian felt compelled to protest.

"I like dancing."

Her eyes flashed. "You would."

Sebastian had no reply to that condemnation.

She wagged a finger at him. "But of greater import is the fact that I do not."

"You might like it with the right partner."

Her expression was pained. "Because I should fall in love and lose my heart forever and just touching the hand of my beloved at intervals would fulfill all the yearning in my soul." She shook her head. "I think not."

What a curious conversation.

"I think you read too much," he ventured to suggest.

"I think you read too little, but such opinions are irrelevant to the discussion at hand."

Sebastian was not accustomed to being chided— much less to having an attractive woman frown and avert her gaze in his presence, her attention clearly not upon him. "Well, my views might be of import as you are asking for my help."

"There is that." She put down the book with a frown and continued solemnly. "This is truly about Daphne. Now that they have two sons, she wishes to be entertained and the duke wishes to see her entertained. She desires to go to London and he wishes to make her happy."

"Is that not a husband's role?"

Miss Eurydice exhaled in exasperation but ignored that comment. "Giving me a season is simply an excuse." She glared at him, as fierce as a kitten. "I decline to be an excuse."

"Most young ladies would be delighted to be given a debut season," Sebastian felt compelled to note. "Especially one funded by a duke inclined to be generous."

Her expression was pained. "Surely you do not imagine that I am like most young ladies?"

"No. Certainly not. You are...most unique."

Instead of giving her pleasure, his comment made her sign in despair. "Truly, sir, I thought you had been given an education. I cannot be *most* unique, or *very* unique or *utterly* unique. It is not possible."

"Whyever not?"

"Because the word 'unique' is one of the few adjectives in the English language that cannot take a modifier. Something is unique or it is not. It is that simple."

"Ah. I shall consider myself to have learned something this day, then."

Miss Eurydice slipped off the desk and retrieved her book. "I had feared you might decline to be useful. How disappointing to be right." She turned to leave the library and Sebastian felt he had to defend himself.

"What exactly would you have me do?"

"You do not want to know."

"I do! In fact, I burn with curiosity."

"You do not."

"Do not underestimate your ability to confound a man, Miss Eurydice."

She smiled then, facing him with consideration in her eyes. "But you will not do it."

"You might be surprised." He leaned forward, bracing his elbows upon his knees to watch her. He smiled. "And you will never know unless you ask me."

"There is that." She marched to the door and he thought she meant to leave. Instead, she closed it firmly, pivoted and impaled him with a glance. "Marry me."

Sebastian nearly fell off his chair. As it was, he considered the possibility that he had imbibed too much brandy and was imagining the conversation. He checked the glass and the bottle while Miss Eurydice watched, then met her gaze with a frown. "Marry you?" he repeated.

"You need not look so surprised. I thought all women wanted to marry you and you think all women are the same. You have a fortune of reasonable size, a title and are not so difficult to look upon."

Sebastian found himself mildly insulted. "I thank you for that."

She shook a finger at him. "But what should be different about this match is that it would not affect either of us in any material sense. It would solely be convenient."

"I cannot imagine there is anything convenient about having a wife." He certainly could not conceive that there would be anything convenient about having Miss Eurydice as a spouse. Doubtless, she would challenge his assumptions each and every day thereafter...

Which did promise to be interesting. Hmm.

"But I do not mean to be a wife, not in that sense." Her becoming blush made her meaning clear.

Sebastian was fascinated. "What other sense is there?"

"The legal one. We would wed and you would reside in your house in Mayfair. You would live as always you do, and people will be scandalized, as always they are by your deeds, and you would be content."

He blinked at this uncommon suggestion. "And you?"

"And I would retire to your country house." She straightened in sudden shock. "You do have one, don't you?" she asked with concern. "One with a library?"

Sebastian smiled. "I do have one, in Cornwall. It has a very nice library as I recall. Even some books. Maps, too, I believe, and the most enormous fireplace."

"Cornwall! Oh, that is even better."

"How so?"

"There are pirates in Cornwall, or tales of them, and, best of all, it is very far from London. You would not be able to visit often at all and I should not be obliged to go to town often, due to the expense and inconvenience."

"But..."

"When did you last visit your country house?" she demanded pertly.

"It has easily been three years. Perhaps four."

"Exactly. It will be perfect!" She smiled at him as if he had been responsible for all the marvels of the world. "We could be wedded before Christmas."

"I am not going to marry you..."

"Whyever not? It will make no difference to your life except to save you from uncomfortable situations. You will always have the excuse that you are married already."

There was something to that argument, but Sebastian feared he was being beguiled. "But people will expect that we have a child," he protested.

"Many couples do not have children." Miss Eurydice sighed. "If you so desire it, I suppose we could discuss that matter at some later date. The fact is that I simply do not have time to bear a child right now. I need to finish my first book and there is so much yet to learn."

Sebastian stood up and shook his head, frowning down at the hopeful maiden. "This is madness."

"But I thought you of all men would be prepared to abandon convention." She shook her head and that curl danced, inviting his touch. "I must say that I am disappointed."

"Which particular convention should I have

abandoned?"

"That you would ask me to wed you, not the other way around. But you would not have thought of it, you see, so I had to make the suggestion."

"I see." He looked at her, waiting with such obvious anticipation for his agreement. What did they say about opportunities that seemed too good to be true? "And all you wish from this arrangement is to live at my country house?"

"Well, I should need some funds settled upon me," she said.

"Aha!"

"But it could be arranged that any provision would only come to me upon your death."

"I do not intend to die soon."

She shook her head solemnly. "No one does. That is why I would need an inheritance that could not be taken away after your demise. While you live, I am certain you would allow me funds to survive."

Sebastian recalled then that the parents of Daphne and Eurydice had died suddenly when the sisters were young. Armstrong must have told him of it. And their grandmother, of course, had been laid to rest the previous summer. It was only reasonable that she thought of practicalities for she had witnessed the changes that occurred after a death firsthand.

He was unaccountably relieved. For a moment, he had thought her a mercenary and worse, he had never guessed she had that trait. She was not avaricious, simply practical.

"It might be wise for me to have a sensible wife," he mused aloud without meaning to do as much. He never could be bothered with accounts, but left it to his estate manager.

She smiled so brightly that he blinked again. "Then we are resolved?"

"No, we are not resolved," Sebastian said with exasperation. "Even if it might be sensible for me to have a practical wife, I have little interest in sense or practicality..."

"I do not believe as much," Miss Eurydice interjected, but he carried on as if she had not spoken.

"I have no intention of wedding at all, and if I did, it would not be..." He faltered then, not wanting to hurt her feelings.

"It would not be to me," she supplied readily. She leaned over and examined the address on the letter he had received that morning. "It would be an actress or a courtesan, an infamous beauty of copious charms." She tapped the return address on the letter. "Someone like Miss Esmeralda Ballantyne."

"Not a courtesan."

"No? Once again, your conventionality surprises me, sir." Her eyes were sparkling in a most unexpected manner. Was she teasing him? Sebastian wondered how he had failed to note her charm sooner. "I should think a courtesan would have suited you perfectly for a wife." She shrugged. "Until, of course, you tired of her charms. I suppose you mean to hasten back to town to Miss Ballantyne." Her expression was innocent but those sparkling eyes hinted that she had seen through him.

"I am just writing to her, to end our arrangement," he admitted without intending to do as much.

Miss Eurydice laughed. "Your page is blank, sir. When did you begin?"

"I do not know what to say," he admitted and pushed a hand through his hair. "I do not wish to provoke her tears..."

Miss Eurydice urged him aside. "I shall show you how useful our agreement will be," she said, to his utter mystification. She urged him aside, then sat down in his place and dipped the quill into the ink. "My dear Miss Ballantyne," she said as she wrote the same words on the page. Her handwriting was not as he might have expected, but neat and economical. It could not have passed for his own but it was not frilly, like Esmeralda's writing. "Thank you for your missive, which arrived this morning. I delighted in your tidings from town. I have happy news of my own to share with you, although admittedly you may not share my joy. I have become betrothed to Miss Eurydice Goodenham while enjoying the duke's hospitality at Airdfinnan, and we will be wed here in Scotland before the Yule. I will escort my bride to my country house—" she looked up, a question in her gaze.

Had he ever seen eyes of such remarkable color?

There were flecks of gold and green and brown within them.

"Rockmorton Manor," Sebastian supplied.

She looked down at her work again and continued to write. "...Rockmorton Manor immediately after the nuptials. We will celebrate the Yule there together, and I will not return to London until March at the earliest. I do hope that you remain well, sincerely etc. etc."

She put down the quill and looked up at him, her expression triumphant. "You see how useful a bride can be?"

"It is in your handwriting."

"I daresay you can copy it. How complete *was* your education?"

"Minx!" Sebastian said and she laughed so merrily that he thought of kissing her to silence.

"Well?" she prompted.

"I shall ponder the suggestion," he said, knowing he would not be able to do otherwise. "I thank you for your consideration, Miss Eurydice."

"You need not be overly flattered," she said as she walked to the door. "I had need of a scoundrel who could be relied upon to keep his word, and you are the only one of my acquaintance."

Sebastian shook his head, unable to keep from smiling at that. "I suppose you will consider that kismet."

She laughed again. "I could only do as much if I believed in love conquering all. No, sir, I think it only a stroke of fortune, and I hope it is one we will act upon." She smiled at him, as fetching a sight as he could imagine, then swept out the door, leaving Sebastian Montgomery with much more to consider than he might have anticipated just an hour before.

Marriage.

To Miss Eurydice.

It was a notion that should have filled him with dread, but Sebastian had the sense it might provide precisely the adventure he sought.

She certainly was not predictable, and she would not expect him to be smitten with her.

It sounded perfect.

It was a beginning.

In fact, Eurydice thought the presentation of her suggestion had gone rather well. The earl had been surprised, of course, but she had not expected otherwise. He had not refused out of hand, but had seemed to be intrigued.

She would not consider her own reaction to his interest. That was simply nature at work. Of course, the warmth in his gaze as he surveyed her had made her pulse leap a little. Of course, she had found it difficult to catch her breath when he stood up and loomed over her a little. He was so much larger and stronger than she, so very muscled and trim. He was handsome—indeed, he could not have been so successful a rake and rogue otherwise. Her reaction was almost enough to make her regret her condition of a marriage in name only. What would it be like to meet a man abed? To be kissed? The very prospect prompted the most delicious shivers.

At least she had left the matter open to negotiation. At the time, she had done as much only to keep him from refusing outright, but she wondered what it would be like to have the earl's hands upon her. They were strong hands, long-fingered and tanned, graceful and yet able with a delicate sensibility. They matched his mouth, which could draw in a taut line of resolve or curve upward unexpectedly into a rakish grin.

She supposed that if they wed, there might be a kiss to seal their vows. That would satisfy some of her curiosity to be sure. And it would be sufficient, perhaps, to allow her to move beyond such seductive notions and complete her book.

She must ask him more about Rockmorton Manor and its library.

How curious that her heart was racing as she descended the great stairs for dinner that night. It was simply a meal, as dinner had been these past four months since the earl's arrival. But there was a tingle within her this night, for Eurydice's proposal had provoked a change.

It was only sensible to be curious as to how much of a change it made.

Eurydice entered the drawing room, only to discover that she was early. She could hear Daphne coming down the stairs, bringing the boys to say goodnight. She was carrying Edmond while Malcolm insisted on descending the long staircase himself. Alexander had to be in his library, for there was a light in there. She moved to the window to watch the ceaseless fall of rain.

"There is a quibble," the earl whispered, his voice so soft and low that the sound gave Eurydice shivers.

She spun to find him lounging in a wing chair immediately behind her. It faced the window, which was why she had not seen him. As ever, he was impeccably dressed in dark trousers and a dark jacket, a white shirt and perfectly tied cravat. His hair was so dark that it seemed to gleam blue, like a raven's wing, and his dark eyes were filled with mysteries. His waistcoat was a rich deep blue silk, embroidered with gold. He looked wicked and gloriously handsome, which had to be why her heart leapt for her throat.

"A quibble?" she managed to say, wondering all the while what had seized her wits earlier in the day. What had made her imagine this was a man who would keep his word?

"Perhaps more than that," he said with apparent regret. His eyes were sparkling, though, and she did not trust him at all. "You see, I must have an heir."

"That was not part of the proposal."

"But I think it must be."

"We agreed to review the question later..."

"We did not agree. You made the suggestion, no more than that." The earl shook his head and rose to his feet, towering over her once again. "But I believe it is a matter we must negotiate in advance, to ensure that we have a right understanding before it is too late." His gaze was warm and he was very close, his watchfulness and the topic at hand making Eurydice feel fluttery.

"An heir. Must it be a boy?"

His brows rose. "I should think so."

"But if we had a daughter first, that would mean the conception of *two* children."

"If not more," he agreed, a smile curving his lips. He leaned closer and whispered. "Do you not expect that I will ensure your enjoyment?"

Eurydice frowned at him and retreated a step, declining to be charmed. "I have no doubt you would ensure that the conception was a merry matter, but I have attended my sister at two deliveries. That part can scarce be worth a night's pleasure."

"It cannot be all bad."

"I assure you it is wretched."

He watched her closely. "Then why did the duchess bear a second child? The first was a son. They could have stopped."

Eurydice shook her head. "They are in love. There is no telling what madness they find reasonable."

The earl laughed, clearly surprised into it. His laughter prompted the duke to pause on the threshold and look. The earl forced himself to sober again just as Daphne arrived in the foyer and

Malcolm shouted for his father. The earl's eyes, though, were filled with a beguiling merriment. "You do not believe in love, then?" he murmured.

"I believe that what many call love is truly lust, and fades with time." Eurydice frowned. "Or possibly with earthly satisfaction." She risked a glance at the earl, surprised to still find that she had his avid attention. "I would expect *you* to know better."

He grinned. "I am familiar with that situation, to be sure."

Eurydice considered her sister and husband in the foyer, averting her gaze from her companion with an effort. "But I suppose there are some who *do* find love in marriage. I would guess it to be rare. What do you think?"

"That it is fiercely uncommon." He spoke without doubt.

"And thus not a reasonable expectation for anyone."

"No," he said, exhaling the word. He sounded wistful, which surprised her into watching him. His expression changed immediately as if he would hide his thoughts from her and he looked dangerous again. "Although many maidens do hope for it, by my understanding."

Eurydice wanted him to be certain of her expectations. "Not I. I think one must be prepared to sacrifice a great deal for such a situation, and that in the end, it might not be so happy after all. Think of Lady Anthea and how she was prepared to wed the baron, even when he was not going to be a baron." She shook her head at the whimsy of the duke's sister.

"You do not think they would have been happy?"

"I believe that Mr. Haskell's concerns were valid. Even if one sacrifices much for love, one may not even achieve that happy state in the end. So much relies upon the other party." She shook her head again, more resolute now. "I would prefer to concentrate on my own efforts and what results I can make from them."

"Your writing."

She smiled, glad that he understood her. "Which may come to naught, to be sure, but I enjoy it so."

He smiled and her heart skipped again. "Then it is worth the endeavor."

Eurydice rushed on. "I would never expect that my husband, especially if our match was an agreement to suit convenience, would lose his heart to me. In fact, I should be disappointed if he so lost his wits."

The earl nodded. "What if we agree that we shall not attempt to conceive an heir for one year after our nuptials are celebrated?"

"One year." Eurydice considered this. She could write a good deal in a year of solitude and comfort. Perhaps she might even compose a second book in that time. "But there is another consideration, sir."

"Is there?"

She drew herself up primly, disliking that she had

to make her objection aloud. "You have had many companions of a most intimate nature," she said, knowing she sounded prim. "An heir is one matter, sir, but you will not give me—" she lowered her voice "—the French disease."

He blinked, looked away, and seemed to be at a loss for words.

"I know that women are not to speak of such matters, but the duke has some very interesting medical treatises in his library, even with illustrations, and I have taken the opportunity to become informed."

That seemed to restore his good humor for some reason, for when he met her gaze again, his eyes were dancing. "Since you are so informed, I would welcome you to examine my person. Is there not a telling rash in such instances of infection?"

Eurydice glared at him even as her cheeks seemed to have taken fire. "You must see a physician, one who will certify that you are not so infected."

"That would be so much less interesting than submitting to your own examination. And I would be delighted to improve upon your education. There are those who would say that book-learning is a distant second to experience." He was enjoying himself overmuch, to Eurydice's thinking.

She found herself sounding stern as a result. "That will not be necessary, sir. I would put my trust in the word of a reputable physician."

He mused upon that. "But I could become so in

that year, by your own reasoning."

"Then, sir, you will have to abstain from such pleasures before you come to my bed. After we have our heir, you can do as you will."

"Abstain?" The earl was visibly shocked. "For an entire year? That is madness..."

"Those are my terms, sir."

"I make you an offer, Miss Eurydice, that I should see the physician and if you find his word acceptable, we will wed and begin the challenge of creating an heir immediately."

"When should I write my book then?"

"After the bundle of joy arrives, of course. You will have years of leisure once your duty to my lineage is fulfilled."

"I think not," Eurydice said, thinking of the change in her sister after the birth of her first son. Daphne had always liked sums and had helped *Grandmaman* with the accounts. After the arrival of her first boy, though, she had abandoned that task for an entire year. It seemed her thoughts were consumed with the marvels of son and husband.

Eurydice dared not risk her book's future.

She noticed that the earl was watching her closely and knew he was tempted by her offer. She recalled the duke's conviction that his old friend liked both a challenge and a gamble and resolved to give him one.

"How disappointing. I thought we came to terms." She straightened as if overcoming a setback. "But do not fear for me, sir. London is awash in rogues. Perhaps I will find one during my season. Or perhaps I will be wedded to a man sufficiently rich to possess a library. I do not even care if he has a title."

"You would wed a tradesman? Or a solicitor?"

"If he had sufficient funds for a library, of course."

The earl's dark brow rose. "Just not the pox."

"Precisely." Eurydice smiled that he understood her priorities. "Perhaps the suggestion of a season is of merit, after all." And she left the earl then, staring after her, as she joined her sister and the duke. She bent down to address their oldest son, as if the earl did not exist. It was a bold play and one that made her heart clamor in fear that she had miscalculated.

Eurydice had chosen on impulse, hoping the dare would be sufficient.

Fortunately, it was not long before she was proven to be right.

CHAPTER TWO

Sebastian let Miss Eurydice worry about his decision.

At least that was his strategy. He sincerely hoped that she was worried about it, but she gave no indication at dinner that she was concerned in the least. In fact, she might have forgotten his existence completely.

It was not how Sebastian preferred women of interest to respond to his presence, much less his attempts to charm. He spoke to Miss Eurydice repeatedly at dinner, but she gave only the barest acknowledgement of his comments, as if she humored him. Armstrong was mightily amused, Sebastian could see as much, and the duchess appeared to be puzzled by his attentions to her sister.

There was no opportunity to speak with Miss

Eurydice after the meal, for she professed herself to be bored with cards and chose to retire early, declaring her anticipation of finishing a most wonderful book.

It had to be the first time that Sebastian had lost a lady's attention to a work of fiction, and he did not welcome the change.

"I suppose you are anxious to return to town," Armstrong said when the two men were left sipping their brandies before the fire. "You have utterly exhausted the possibility of conquest at Airdfinnan."

"Do you think so?"

"Attempting to charm Eurydice is a true mark of desperation. She has not a romantic fiber in her being, and no interest in men at all, as far as I have noticed." Armstrong shrugged. "I thought that might change as she grew older, but I perceive no difference. Daphne believed that the prospect of a season would pique her interest."

"I will wager it has not."

Armstrong shook his head.

"She does not seem to be the kind of young lady who is tempted by a shopping expedition, unless it is for books," Sebastian suggested and Armstrong laughed.

"Precisely so. But it is of no matter."

"How can it be of no matter whether she marries or not?"

"She has no fortune, less than fifty pounds per year, but I gave my promise to her grandmother that

I would always ensure her welfare, whether she chose to wed or not." Armstrong gestured to the full bookshelves. "She is more than content here and when she has read them all, I have no doubt she will present me with a list of suitable acquisitions. She charms the children and is no trouble to have in the house at all. She is not demanding, she does not have expensive taste, and indeed, it is easy to forget her presence entirely."

Sebastian frowned. He could not overlook Miss Eurydice's presence and never imagined he would again. "It seems a meager bargain on her side."

"Does it? Comfort, shelter, good food and all the books she desires? I would wager that Miss Eurydice thinks the matter most neatly resolved." Armstrong drained his glass and set it down. "Now I will say goodnight." He yawned but the gesture was so obviously contrived that Sebastian smiled.

"You need not feign exhaustion to me," he charged with a smile. "Even I have been in residence long enough to know that the duchess will have had time to retire to her chamber by now."

Armstrong's grin was quick and wicked. "I did not wish to make you aware of what you were missing. Why didn't you bring Miss Ballantyne?"

"And scandalize all of Scotland?"

"You enjoy scandalizing everyone."

"But Miss Ballantyne has no affection for hunting, country houses, Scotland or rain." Sebastian shrugged, realizing how very discontent Esmeralda tended to be when matters were not to her taste. She could be a gem, but was only one that sparkled in its favored setting. "Better she remained in comfort in London."

"Then you should have told me in advance and I would have found some other eligible ladies to invite. I daresay the Dempsters could arrive in a fortnight if invited now."

"Do not trouble yourself on my account," Sebastian said. "I will have departed by then." He stood up, setting down his own empty glass, and smiled at his old friend. "I would not wish to wear out my welcome."

"Never!" Armstrong declared and they left the library together, each to retire to his own rooms. Considering what awaited him there, Sebastian made a detour to the library to choose a book.

If he was going to wed Eurydice, he had best become familiar with her pleasures.

He was standing before the bookshelves before he wondered precisely what kind of book she was writing herself.

❧❧

"A year is utterly impossible."

Eurydice jumped at the sound of the earl's low voice. She was in the dining room the following morning, content to be alone at breakfast, for she had the duke's London newspaper. It was three days old, but she expected to be able to devour every line before anyone else appeared. She alone was an early riser in the household, though she sometimes heard the children in the nursery when she emerged from her bedroom.

The dining room at Airdfinnan had a high ceiling and large windows on three sides. On a glorious autumn day like this one promised to be, it was bathed in golden sunlight. Eurydice had eaten her eggs and had a full pot of fresh tea, as well as that newspaper. This room, all to herself, combined with the other pleasures of the day was her notion of paradise.

Though she could not deny that the earl's appearance improved it yet more.

"You do not customarily come down for breakfast so early," she said, realizing too late that she sounded rude.

He was loading a plate from the sideboard and she took the opportunity to survey him while his attention was diverted. He truly had fine legs. He turned quickly, surprising her, and smiled when she averted her gaze. "Should I confess that I was awake all the night long, considering your challenge?"

"Only if that is true."

"It is not. I slept admirably." He took the place opposite her and she poured him a cup of tea. He nodded his thanks and began to eat, craning his neck to read the headlines on her newspaper.

As he seemed disinclined to continue, Eurydice had to ask. "Then why are you awake so early?"

"Because I slept so well. I retired in a timely manner, instead of spending much of the night— and morning—carousing, gambling and womanizing." He lowered his voice and gave her a devilish look. "There is a wretched lack of women at Airdfinnan."

"At least those of the easy virtue you so admire."

He did not seem insulted by the barb. "Exactly. Which is why I will return to town on the morrow." He wagged his knife at her. "The question is whether I shall be betrothed or not when I leave."

Eurydice's heart skipped a beat, then lodged in her throat. He was watching her with a knowing expression in his eyes and that cursed smile, the one that made her wonder if he could read her thoughts. "I understood you had declined."

"I understood that we negotiated." He put down his knife and fork and fixed her with a look. "The simple fact is that it would be impossible for me to be celibate for a year. That condition is out of the question."

"What do you suggest then?"

"A month."

Eurydice sputtered in the act of sipping her tea. "A month?! How much could I write in a month?"

"I have no idea, but if you have half the wits I think you do, you should be able to write a great deal that is considerably better than the book I read last night. It was, in fact, responsible for my sound sleep."

"What book?"

The Castle of Otronto." He yawned mightily even as Eurydice gasped in outrage.

"But that is the very foundation of the gothic

novel as we know it today," she said. "You can't possibly have found it wanting..."

"It was dull. And absurd. Fathers marrying their son's betrothed, mysterious knights, enormous heads and far too much racing about in the dark with knives and swords." He shook his head and finished his breakfast, then impaled her with a look. "I have no doubt you can do better."

Eurydice did not know what to say. She was both offended that he had criticized a work she admired and flattered that he thought so highly of her talents. The earl had no basis for such an opinion, to be sure, and Eurydice realized belatedly that he was trying to charm her. That took the power from his words.

She glared at him. "You, sir, will use any tactic to win your way, even flattery. One year is my condition and it stands."

Instead of appearing to be dismayed, his eyes twinkled. "But a year is quite impossible, Miss Eurydice. You must see that. How long have I been at Airdfinnan on this visit?"

"Four months."

"You are counting the days!" he teased.

Eurydice felt herself flush. "My sister noted the length of your stay the other day. She wondered whether you were quite well to linger here so long."

He laughed. "In the first week, there was that amiable daughter of the innkeeper in the Finnan Falls..."

"I do not wish to know of your exploits!"

Eurydice protested, both outraged and fascinated.

"But you must, in order to understand the severity of the challenge you place before me."

"It is most uncommon, sir, to recount your exploits..."

"But we have left convention well and truly behind, Miss Eurydice," the earl countered with a look. Eurydice was compelled to nod agreement and he continued. "And in the second week, the newest maid of the household saw fit to entertain me one morning." He smiled like a cat that has found the cream. "Now there is a fine way to begin the day..."

"Sir!"

In the morning?

Why had Eurydice never thought of that?

"Almost as good as a lazy afternoon abed, in my experience," he confided and she blinked. "I shall spare you the intervening details, and hasten to the most recent incident. Two weeks ago, Baron Thornedyke and his wife were here with their twin sons, along with that luscious lady's maid in her service..."

"Cease, sir!" Eurydice protested and he did.

She was not certain whether to be relieved or feel she had only half the tale. She poured more hot tea into her cup then sipped it so quickly that she burned her tongue.

And he knew of her discomfiture, the wretch. His eyes danced as he watched her.

"The point, then, is that it has been nine days, Miss Eurydice. *Nine.*" The earl scanned the room then met her gaze again, his eyes bright. "A month will be a walk through hellfire, but I would endure it to please my bride. A year is utterly out of the question."

Eurydice found herself swayed by his intense expression. "But it is not sufficient time. You must see a doctor and possibly take treatment…"

"I am not ill. I guarantee as much."

"But…"

"But I am not so cavalier as you would believe, Miss Eurydice. I share your concern about illness, to be sure."

Eurydice did not know what to say to that. It was so startling to imagine that they had any common concerns.

The earl leaned across the table to make his appeal, his voice dropping low. Eurydice found her reservations melting beneath his steady gaze. "One night a week, beginning after one month's delay," he suggested. "It is the barest minimum to ensure that I can be monogamous."

"I might conceive right away."

"You might, and then you would be rid of me. You could write all the day and all the night at Rockmorton Manor." There was a glint in his eyes that Eurydice did not entirely trust. "What kind of book are you writing, by the way."

"I can't speak of it. Not until it is done."

"Ah," he said wisely, those eyes glinting.

"You have a scheme," she accused.

"It would be fair to say that you had a scheme

first."

She laughed, for that was true, and he watched her, a warmth in his dawning smile that fed an answering heat within herself.

Goodness, he was an alluring man.

"I would even let you read my newspapers first," he murmured in a low voice.

Eurydice was shocked by how readily she was tempted. "But if you are near the limit of your tolerance, sir, when should we be wed? And how shall you endure another month?"

His smile flashed. "Is it not reasonable for a man and his betrothed to kiss? It will be like small hors d'oeuvres to whet the appetite before the meal."

The notion of being nibbled by the earl was most distracting. "But, but..."

"But you have only read about such intimacy in books," he guessed, rising from his seat and moving around the table toward her with deliberate grace. Eurydice felt both stalked and thrilled.

"True," she managed to admit even as she stumbled to her own feet. Curiously, she had no urge to flee even though her heart was racing.

The earl halted immediately before her, then lifted a hand. He captured a curl upon her cheek, watching it wind around his fingertip with a smile. Then he touched that warm fingertip to her cheek, ever so gently, launching an army of shivers over her flesh. Eurydice swallowed, amazed at her reaction to that simple caress, and was amazed to find her knees weakening. He was close, so close that she could feel his breath upon her lips, so close that she could have drowned in those dark eyes. "Do we have an agreement, Miss Eurydice?" he murmured.

"But I proposed," she said, hearing that her own voice was breathless. "It is you who must be willing."

"Oh, I am willing, Miss Eurydice, if you accept my terms." He bent and touched his lips to her temple. Eurydice caught her breath and inhaled the clean masculine scent of him, feeling a frisson of pleasure. His lips were firm and warm and she closed her eyes, awash in a most delightful medley of sensation. "Do you?" he murmured and Eurydice feared she would agree to anything just to have his attention.

A month, she forced herself to recall. Then couplings every week thereafter. And otherwise to be left to her own devices. It was a surprisingly small price to pay for the security and freedom she desired and she was not so witless as to let opportunity slip away.

"Of course, sir," she whispered. "I chose you, after all."

The earl laughed then, no more than a surprised exhalation of breath, then his fingers were beneath her chin. She had a glimpse of the expression in his eyes, sparkling with merriment but also tinged with solemnity, before his lashes swept down, hiding his thoughts, and he claimed her mouth with a kiss.

It was a sweet kiss, surprisingly so, a gentle and

cajoling kiss that had Eurydice rising to her toes in a quest for more. Her hands had just landed on his shoulders and his arm had wrapped around her waist when there was a footfall on the threshold.

"Upon my word!" the duke declared, outrage in his tone. "Is this what routinely occurs in my dining room each morning?"

"Of course not," the earl said easily, pivoting to confront his host so that Eurydice was behind him. She felt her cheeks burn and was glad the earl held fast to her hand. "This is the first such happy instance, Your Grace, for Miss Eurydice has accepted my proposal." He gave her fingers a minute squeeze, acknowledging that this was not quite true, but Eurydice knew as well as the earl that the duke would not accept any deviation from convention. She kept silent, fearing Alexander's reaction.

And rightly so.

"You shall not wed!" he declared, striding into the room with purpose. Alexander's customary good nature was utterly lacking and he looked prepared to fight. "Eurydice, would you leave us, please?" he asked tightly when she did not move.

"I would hear this," she protested.

"I think she should hear whatever you have to say," the earl said, holding his ground and her hand.

Alexander glared at them. "I forbid such a match."

"On what grounds?" the earl asked, a challenge in his tone.

The duke's eyes flashed brilliant blue. "It is utterly unsuitable, and if you do not know as much, Eurydice, Montgomery should." He glared at his friend. "A man of any merit would acknowledge that truth."

The earl was unmoved, even by the slight against his nature. Indeed, he smiled. "Perhaps the lady will reform me."

"Perhaps you take advantage where you should not," Alexander retorted. "You and I will discuss this in privacy, immediately." And he abandoned the dining room, marching toward his library with purpose.

"I suppose he must give his permission," Eurydice acknowledged with reluctance.

"Nonsense," her betrothed said with unexpected resolve. "We have an agreement and we will keep it. I advise you to quietly pack your belongings."

"Sir?"

The earl winked. "He will cast me out for such an affront. I will depart immediately thereafter and we shall wed this very day."

"But that is impossible..."

The earl dropped his voice to a dangerous whisper. "It is not. You will meet me at the stables and we will stop at Gretna Green on the route south."

Eurydice's mouth opened and closed again as she stared at him. "But that would be scandalous."

His eyes sparkled. "And what will you write about, Miss Eurydice, if you do not live with adventure?"

Eurydice had no reply to that.

Against every possible expectation, the earl was right.

"And since we are in league together, I believe you should call me Sebastian," he advised as if he had read her thoughts.

"Sebastian," she said softly and liked how he smiled in pleasure. "Eurydice, of course." She curtsied.

"Of course." He bowed, then his wicked gaze dropped to her lips again, he leaned an increment closer—then Alexander shouted a summons, curse him. The earl—Sebastian—retreated a step. He sighed with great forbearance, clearly enjoying that he would set the entire household at odds, and Eurydice could not help but smile. "Make haste," he whispered.

She nodded once and the earl kissed his fingertips, then winked before he bowed again and went to be chastised by the duke. Eurydice scarce could keep from laughing at his manner.

Wicked man. He would lead her astray unless she watched her step.

Gretna Green!

She would not just wed, but would elope. This, indeed, would be an experience to inform her writing.

Eurydice halted on the stairs, struck by an errant thought. Sebastian was a rake and a scoundrel. What if this plan to ride to Gretna Green was a ploy to seduce her and leave her despoiled?

The notion stopped her cold. She did not think that Sebastian was that sort of rogue, but she had never been alone with him. She knew little of such men and could not be certain.

Which only meant that if she was going to put herself in his power by leaving Airdfinnan with him, then she had best be prepared to fend for herself.

She would pack appropriately.

His driver and team had been ready, his valet packed and his portmanteau loaded on the carriage by the time Sebastian was hurled out of Airdfinnan by his old friend, Armstrong. Sebastian could not have planned it better himself.

He had a moment to fear that his intended was one of those women who could not pack with haste when Eurydice darted out of the shadows of the stables. She had her valise in one hand and a black umbrella in the other. She was wearing her boots, bonnet and a dark cloak. She also had a stack of books under her other arm. She looked both resolute and thrilled, errant curls all around her face. Sebastian could not recall when he had last seen such an alluring woman.

He saved the bundle of books before they tumbled to the ground, touching his finger to his lips. He then handed her into the carriage, using the door on the opposite side from the house. His coach was much smaller than either of Armstrong's, but then he usually rode by himself, his staff outside. Once they were settled, he rapped his knuckles on the roof, suspecting that they would make better time than Armstrong could. His team were well-rested, as well as young and vigorous, and the smaller coach was light.

He indicated that Eurydice should take the seat facing backward, and sat in the other himself. The guard on the bridge would think him alone. She evidently planned for the same illusion, for she laid down on the seat to be entirely out of view. He tucked her valise beneath the seat and she put the books on the seat beside her. They were bound together with a belt and he wondered which ones she had not been able to bear leaving behind. The umbrella she gripped like a weapon.

He did not speak until they were over the bridge and Fletcher had cracked the whip. The horses cantered at speed down the lane, making the coach rock.

"Did anyone see you?" he asked, helping her to sit up. Of course, the exercise had allowed half a dozen curls to escape her ribbons.

"No one. They were all trying to listen to the duke without seeming to do so."

"That would not have taken much effort."

She smiled. "He did shout quite loudly. I had no notion he had such a temper."

"Well, the thing with Armstrong is that when he becomes deadly serious, he cannot bear to be teased. It is the surest way to send him into a fury."

She eyed him, her gaze filled with understanding. "You did it on purpose."

"I knew he would not change his mind. The best plan was to provoke him, the better to grant you sufficient time to pack."

She waved a gloved hand. "It was the work of an instant."

"Even choosing which books to bring?"

At that, she winced. "I have a list of the ones I was compelled to leave behind." She reached into the small purse that dangled from her wrist and presented it to him. "Perhaps you might indulge me with their replacement."

Sebastian felt his eyes widen as he scanned the very extensive list. She might prove to be a more expensive wife than he had anticipated. "Perhaps we should check the library at Rockmorton first. We would not wish to have duplicates."

She stared at him. "Don't you know what books are in your library?"

"I haven't the faintest notion. I don't go to the country to *read*, Eurydice."

"You should," she said. "It would be idyllic." She retrieved her list and tucked it away. "It is my sole copy," she informed him.

"I shall consult with you whenever I feel inclined to visit a bookseller," Sebastian said. He meant it to be a jest, but as he said the words, he found the pledge to be utterly reasonable.

She eyed him for a moment, as if uncertain whether to trust his word.

"I will," he vowed.

"Good," she said. "I would not wish you to be waylaid by the books with pictures."

Sebastian might have taken umbrage, but could not do so when her lips twitched so. They watched each other across the bouncing coach for a long moment, then he eased to one side. "You should sit here."

"Is it safe?"

"You are to be my wife."

"But we are not wedded yet, and a month will be a long time for you, to my understanding. I should not wish to tempt you overmuch."

"Too late," he said on impulse, reaching to tuck back one of her curls. He leaned toward her and lowered his voice. "I am only here, Eurydice, because you *have* tempted me."

She flushed crimson but her gaze did not waver. In that moment, Sebastian suddenly understood the appeal of maidens. Indeed, he was looking forward to introducing Eurydice to the pleasures of the flesh. That notion made him smile, which did not pass unobserved.

"You are thinking something wicked," she charged.

"I routinely think wicked things."

"Something particularly wicked. Tell me."

"Or?"

"Or I will not share my realization with you."

"A realization?"

"One key to the success of our plan." She

nodded wisely and he thought perhaps she was bluffing.

He patted the seat. "Come here and I will tell you."

She moved immediately, abandoning her books on the other seat. Her thigh was close to his, thick cloak not hiding that truth at all. Her shoulder bumped his as the coach took a turn and he glanced down to find her watching him. "Well? I am here, sir, as you may have noticed."

Sebastian smiled. "I did notice, to be sure."

"You were thinking something wicked," she prompted.

"I was thinking of how interesting it will be to teach you of the pleasures of the flesh."

She did not smile but eyed him solemnly. "You have never been with a maiden?"

He shook his head. "I have never found innocence alluring."

"Whyever not?" She was genuinely curious.

He averted his gaze, considering the question. "I like to be sure that all parties involved know the implications and ramifications of their choices. Surprises, I find, are unwelcome, particularly in the bedroom."

Her expression turned coy. "You might find me less innocent than you expect."

"Because you have read the medical treatises in Armstrong's library?" Sebastian shook his head and wagged a finger at her. "You may find that experience is vastly different from book knowledge."

"That sounds like we should make a wager," she said, much to his surprise.

"That you will not find the truth better than your anticipation?"

"Oh, it will likely be better, but I doubt it will be different otherwise."

"I would wager otherwise. In fact, I could take that as a challenge."

"You have a month to consider the matter."

Sebastian smiled, knowing already what his choice would be. The coach turned and lurched onto the post road. He checked his watch and thought they were making good time. "We might make Gretna Green tomorrow," he said with some satisfaction.

"But we should not go there," Eurydice said, to his astonishment.

Sebastian stared at her. "Have you changed your thinking? We have an arrangement, if you so recall..."

She touched his sleeve fleetingly, blushed and smiled. "Alexander will expect us to go to Gretna Green."

Sebastian could not argue with that. "Likely."

"He is my guardian and I am not yet twenty-one years of age, and we know that he disapproves of our match." She nodded. "He vigorously disapproves."

"Yes. I cannot imagine what made him so cursedly conservative. Do you think marriage itself is at root? He has always been responsible, but there was a time when he could be relied upon to support harmless mischief."

Eurydice surveyed him so sternly that Sebastian fell silent. "Despoiling his ward is hardly harmless mischief."

"I am not going to despoil you. I am going to marry you! I gave my word!"

"But you can do as much only if Alexander fails to intercede before we exchange our vows." She said this with a satisfaction that Sebastian hardly thought the situation merited. "Which is why we must *not* go to Gretna Green at all."

Sebastian was confused. "So, you would rather be despoiled than married."

"Don't be ridiculous," she chided. "Gretna Green is the obvious choice for a hasty marriage, but the fact of the matter is that our vows must simply be exchanged in *Scotland*. Hardwicke's Marriage Act of 1753 is not law in Scotland and it is that law which prohibits our match, at least for several years yet." She reached for her stack of books, and removed one with an effort. It was a thick tome bound in black leather, which she began to thumb through with haste. "Fortunately, I had been researching the law regarding marriage in England and had this book in my room when you and Alexander began to argue in the library. I brought it along in case it might prove useful."

Why would she be researching marriage law?

Sebastian had no time to ask before she opened

it to a page which included the text of the marriage act in question. She presented it to him proudly. "You see?"

Sebastian stared at the dense page of text, then at her. "You mean we could have just been wed in Finnan village?"

Eurydice shook her head. "That would have been a foolish choice! The pastor in the living granted by the duke would never have wed us against his patron's will. No, that would never have done." She sighed. "Never mind that the duke, as my guardian, could demand that our marriage be annulled, even if we have exchanged our vows, if it had not been consummated. See, here?"

Instead of looking as indicated, Sebastian closed the book and sat back. "So, you *have* changed your mind."

"We have an agreement, sir, and that is to consummate our match in thirty days, after you have visited a physician."

"We cannot outrun Armstrong for a month, no matter where we wed."

"We do not have to," she said calmly. "We must simply evade him."

"It is not that big of an island," he protested and she smiled. "I surrender. What is your scheme now?"

She laughed at him, a most charming sight. "Scotland is a large territory, and one with many churches, sir. We might try the tollhouse at Coldwater or even Lambton. They are in the trade of offering hasty marriages as well as Gretna Green and Alexander will not expect us to journey so far out of our way." She bit her lip, frowning slightly. "And then we must encourage the assumption that our match is consummated. We could take rooms and by the time Alexander finds us, we will have been there some days and nights." She met his gaze steadily. "It will be assumed to be too late for an annulment then."

Sebastian could not think of a single objection to this scheme. "That is sound thinking, Eurydice," he said, not hiding his admiration a whit. She blushed crimson, but he knew she was pleased. "And surely it is deserving of some celebration."

"Celebration?" she managed to say before Sebastian framed her face in one gloved hand, smiled into her eyes, then bent and kissed her soundly.

This time, he was not so cautious as before, but kissed her as he thought a woman should be kissed. To his delight, after Eurydice gasped in surprise, she kissed him back with no small measure of her own enthusiasm.

This unlikely union was showing definite promise.

CHAPTER THREE

Sebastian was dangerous, to be sure.

And his kiss was even more so. This embrace left Eurydice flustered, shaken and utterly thrilled. She had never imagined that a simple kiss—the meeting of two pairs of lips—could be such a marvelous experience. She nearly forgot herself and all her notions of good behavior, nearly flung her arms around his neck and surrendered to pleasure.

Fortunately, she recalled her senses in time and tore her lips from his. She would have been despoiled, for certain, and through no small effort of her own.

For good measure, she retreated to the other side of the carriage and put her books in her lap. When she looked up, Sebastian was smiling at her.

Surely he could not have a scheme of seduction?

"I thought you were a maiden in search of adventure," he said, a thread of humor in his voice. Was he teasing her or revealing his plan? Eurydice could not see his eyes for he occupied himself with his snuffbox.

"I thought your word had merit, but feared just then that I had been mistaken."

He looked up quickly, so quickly that she saw his surprise. "We will be wed," he said tightly, as if insulted. "I gave my word."

"Then you will not be troubled if I insist that all demonstrations of affection wait until that happy objective is achieved." Eurydice sounded pompous and she knew it, but she had feared that she had judged him mistakenly.

Sebastian wagged a finger at her. "I agreed upon thirty days, but you must allow some crumbs from the table."

"Must I?"

He frowned then. "It was merely a kiss," he said, as if it had been nothing at all.

Eurydice suddenly felt her innocence quite keenly. "Not to me," she said.

"Truly?" His eyes lit with familiar devilry. "Then perhaps there is hope for me yet."

Eurydice regarded him with suspicion. "What is that to mean?"

He smiled and leaned closer, removing her books from her lap and setting them on the seat beside her. "That you appear to be the sole woman of my acquaintance who is unswayed by my charm."

Eurydice found herself fighting a smile. "The sole one?"

He nodded solemnly but she did not believe him for a moment. "You must see that the situation is provocative."

"It is hardly provocative!"

"Oh, but it is. I am tempted to take the challenge of winning your approval." He took her hand and pressed a kiss to its back, looking up so suddenly that she was snared by his wicked expression. "Perhaps even endeavor to steal your heart."

Eurydice pulled her hand from his grasp. "Ours is a purely practical arrangement."

"That does not mean it must be entirely...bland."

"What manner of spice do you seek?"

He smiled then, leaving no doubt of his meaning.

"You cannot win my heart," Eurydice said firmly, even as she wondered whether it might be done. If only he had not been so very handsome, and confident, and charming...

"All the more reason to try," Sebastian replied. "I must occupy myself with some task for thirty days, to be sure."

"You might read some books," Eurydice countered. "I could offer some recommendations."

"I have no doubt that you could. I could read yours."

"No," she said flatly for it was not fit to be shown to anyone yet.

"Should I be insulted that you trust me so little?"

"It is not fit for anyone to read as yet."

"Ah." His eyes widened and she knew he would try to make her laugh. "Would that medical treatise you found in Armstrong's library be amongst your recommendations?"

"It might encourage your interest in monogamy," she replied. "There were *illustrations*."

Sebastian grimaced, dismissing this, then fixed her with a playful look. "But would you truly desire my undivided attention? I thought the premise of this arrangement was that we would each pursue our own lives, unencumbered by the expectations of the other."

"Of course, it is. But you cannot wish to visit a physician monthly."

"Not part of the wager, my dear Eurydice. I will go once, this very month, as agreed." He leaned forward again, that challenge in his eyes. "Perhaps I should try to steal your heart away, so we might be so consumed with each other that this marriage becomes a real one in every way."

"Do not tell me that you are a romantic, sir!"

"Can you not believe it?"

Eurydice shook her head. "Surely you of all men cannot believe in the merit of love?"

"Quite the opposite," he assured her solemnly. "Because I have seen true love and felt its power. When it is gone, the void cannot be filled." Before she could ask, his gaze brightened and his tone became less serious. "But what of you? Are not all maidens romantics, particularly those who wish to write books?"

Sebastian a romantic. Eurydice would never have expected as much. Had someone broken his heart? What kind of woman had she been? Why had she abandoned him? There was a tale Eurydice would like to hear.

"True love is nonsense," she said. "And love at first sight even more so." She was forced to make a concession beneath his bright gaze. "Although, both make for good stories."

He laughed. "Do you not think of life as a story? I consider myself to be living the tale of my life: whenever the telling of it might bore an attentive reader, I know that I must do something outrageous to enliven the tale."

Eurydice stared at him in surprise. "That is a most compelling perspective," she had to admit.

He bowed his head slightly. "I thank you. And what is your creed of life?"

"Only that there is insufficient time to read all the books, so I must make use of every moment."

"To read or to live?"

Eurydice hesitated. "I had thought to read."

"But reading of an experience is hardly the same as living it oneself," Sebastian argued. "I vote for living each day to its fullest. I will read in my dotage when I have not the strength to enliven my own tale."

"I doubt that day will come soon."

"I hope it never comes, but in the meantime, Miss Goodenham, do tell me why you don't believe in true love."

He watched her, smiling slightly, as the coach rocked. Eurydice heard the hoof beats of the horses and the calls of the driver, the creak of the leather seats and the jingle of the trap. She could not look away from the dark splendor of Sebastian's eyes, though, or evade the impression that he would wait forever for her confession.

She cleared her throat finally. "My parents' marriage was arranged, as was that of my grandparents. I daresay their affection grew over time, but the initial impulse was practical. They were good candidates, each for the other. I admire the practicality in that."

Sebastian nodded, his gaze straying to the window. "And what of your sister's match?"

Eurydice stifled the urge to wince. "The original impulse was inarguably a material one."

She had Sebastian's undivided attention then, his eyes as bright as those of a cat. "How so? I thought they were immediately smitten, each with the other."

"Daphne was always determined to wed a duke. I believe the matter was settled in her mind the moment she saw the crest upon his coach." She watched Sebastian's expression become inscrutable and wondered at his own views. "They may say it was love at first, but I am skeptical."

Sebastian nodded thoughtfully. No doubt he was troubled to find himself alone in his views. "The duke's sister and the baron?" he invited.

"They were companions one summer at Airdfinnan in their youth and came to like each other well when there was no mention of marriage at all. I would call them friends who became more affectionate in time."

He tilted his head to study her. "Then you do not believe in true love?"

"Not as it is presented in tales, a grand sweeping passion that compels its victims to forget all else." She meant to be mocking but the earl did not smile.

"But what if I could change your mind?" he asked softly.

Eurydice laughed. "By persuading me to fall in love with you? I am far too sensible for that, sir."

He leaned back, his eyes dark. "And there, you have offered the challenge to fill my every waking hour for the next month."

"It cannot be done."

"Even better. I so dislike an objective easily won." He smiled, his confidence so supreme that Eurydice could only shake her head in amusement at him.

"And what of your heart? Will you tell me your tale of lost love?"

"That is not the matter at hand," he said firmly, then patted the seat beside him, changing the subject. "If you are so impervious to my so-called charm, then there is naught to be risked by sitting beside me."

Eurydice looked at him. She saw that he was issuing a challenge of his own, and she impulsively chose to take it. She moved across the carriage with purpose, but her move coincided with the couch taking a turn. She lost her balance and tumbled into Sebastian's lap, only to find his arms around her waist and his knowing gaze all too close. "Now that is how a dare should be accepted," he murmured, his gaze dropping to her lips.

Eurydice twisted free and dropped to the seat beside him, sparing him a glare. "If you try to despoil me, I will ensure you regret it," she whispered with heat.

"Which is why I would never dream of doing as much," he said lightly. "You are precisely the kind of person who would never forget to avenge a wrong done against her."

Eurydice was intrigued. "How do you know that?"

"Because you are so serious of nature, Eurydice. In that, we are complete opposites."

She twisted to look at him, not wanting to miss any change in his expression. "Are we?"

"Do you doubt it?"

"I think you contrive an appearance, perhaps to keep curiosity at bay. I confess that I come to wonder what lies behind your mask."

His gaze flicked then he smiled again. "A pity, then, that we are to have a marriage of convenience and live at such great distance from each other." He winked. "By your own choice, as well, so you cannot complain of the bargain."

Eurydice frowned, sensing she had lost

something of merit. "You are vexing, sir."

He laughed again, his usual mood restored. "It is, I regret, a habit of long standing." Then he turned his attention to the view, leaving her thoughts swirling with unanswered questions.

Would he try to convince her to fall in love with him?

It was only sensible that she wished to know who had stolen his heart—and why that person was no longer in his company. If anything, the confession made him more fascinating than before. She had been so certain that Sebastian had no secrets or hidden sides to his nature.

And now, she yearned to know them all.

She doubted he would relinquish them readily.

There was little Sebastian liked better than to challenge expectations. If Eurydice suspected that he meant to despoil and abandon her, he would undermine her assessment of his character by being a perfect gentleman.

When she fell asleep on his shoulder in the late afternoon, he did not steal a kiss or even as much as a caress. Indeed, he abandoned his favored seat, rolling his jacket into a pillow for her, and tucking her cloak around her so she could sleep beneath his watchful eye. Her suspicions made him into a nursemaid. When they finally halted for the night at an inn that was not nearly far enough from the main road for comfort, he secured the last available room for her before urging her awake.

"I told them you were my sister," he whispered when her eyes opened. "And en route to a convent. They agreed that you could go up the back stairs, the better to avoid being seen by the men in the tavern."

He pulled her hood over her face before ushering her into the inn and sheltered even the servants' view of her with his body. When she was in the small room with a single candle, he bade her lock the door while he fetched her a meal.

"Must you have a maid?" he asked with a wince. "It would leave a witness of your presence."

She frowned, looking disheveled and adorably sleepy. Her gaze darted to the dark window. "Do you think he will..."

He laid a finger across her lips to silence her, then bent to whisper in her ear. "We are not far from the main road. We may be caught up before dawn, but the horses had to stop."

"Then surely his will, as well."

"He might have taken a change of horses." Their gazes held for a long moment, and Sebastian knew she understood that the depth of Armstrong's concern for her welfare would govern that man's choices.

"And what of you?"

"I will sleep in the tavern, in my cloak. This is the last remaining room." He glanced around. "Indeed, it might be the only one."

"But..."

Again, Sebastian silenced her with a touch. "I keep my promises, upon that you can rely." He stared into her eyes until she nodded, glad to see a little smile of pleasure curve her lips. "Three raps on the door will be me with dinner," he whispered. "Unlock it to no others."

She nodded agreement and Sebastian left her in the dreary little chamber. He heard the key turn in the lock when he was on the stairs.

It was almost half an hour later when he returned, accompanied by a maid who would not be left behind. She carried a steaming bowl of stew, while Sebastian had the small jug of ale and a hot brick wrapped in flannel. He made a show of talking loudly to the maid on the stairs and to his relief, a hooded Eurydice met them at the door. She was clever, both to disguise her identity and to ensure that the maid did not hear his signal.

He would have liked to have lingered and spoken to her, perhaps reviewed their plan for the morning, but the maid was attentive, and in the end, he left with the girl. Again, he heard the key turn in the lock and dared to be reassured.

It was much later that he realized he should have known better.

Sebastian spent a long night awkwardly sleeping in a chair with his cloak wrapped around himself. The locals drank ale in the tavern until the wee hours of the morning, singing heartily near the end, which made an early retirement impossible. He spent those hours thinking of Eurydice and the challenges she offered, endeavoring to itemize them all.

She did not find him alluring.

She was not charmed by him.

She did not believe in love.

He sincerely doubted she had any intention of loving him, ever.

Despite the practical nature of their arrangement, Sebastian found this prospect troubling. It was not just new and unwelcome. At issue was not just that he was unaccustomed to women being disinterested in him, but that he was increasingly interested in Eurydice Goodenham. He was already fond of her. He liked her very much and was sorely tempted to convince her to love him.

For his own side, Sebastian did not believe in the merit of a practical marriage. His parents had been besotted with each other, having fallen in love at first glance. They had defied the expectations of their families to elope together, then had made steady progress together in overcoming each and every objection to their match. Their love had been the bedrock of their lives, unshakeable from that first meeting. They had been fearsome when united in purpose, indomitable together as they could never be alone. Indeed, it was the lofty ideal of their partnership and the romance behind it that persuaded Sebastian to live alone for the duration. He would not compromise for a pale shadow of what he knew was possible, so he would do without.

But then there was Eurydice Goodenham.

In the shadows of the tavern, he acknowledged why he had accepted her challenge. For the novelty of it, to be sure, and the very audacity of her making such a suggestion—and because she intrigued him in every possible way. At the time, he had made the excuse to himself that it was a fine disguise for the life he meant to live, but the truth was he had recognized her as the only woman he could love. He was in peril of being the sole person in love in his marriage, thus by every passing hour, he wondered more what it would be like to capture Eurydice's heart.

How could the feat be done?

How could he claim her heart and keep her respect?

Was it even possible for Eurydice to fall madly in love? Sebastian could not be certain, which was troubling indeed.

Why love her? Sebastian had no doubt that she would fight savage beasts for any person she held in affection. She was fierce in her loyalty, to be sure, and absolute in her choices—yet she was not predictable. He could imagine awakening each day, wondering what she would say or do next to enchant him. She was clever and he liked how they solved issues together. Her quick wits had already proven an asset. Once an ally, she would never be shaken from one's side.

But would she ever trust him so much as that?

Sebastian could not imagine that she would ever be so foolish. Would she come to love another man in time? That was a troubling possibility. He would have to ensure that no sober and responsible gentlemen ever crossed her path if he meant to have any hope of claiming her heart.

But how could he do as much if she was in Cornwall while he was in London? There was a puzzle he could not readily solve.

There was no doubt about it—Eurydice was more adept at challenging his expectations than any person Sebastian had ever met before.

And that was the heart of the matter, to be sure.

What a vexing man.

Sebastian's inconsistencies were wretchedly annoying and that made him distracting as well. Eurydice sat in her room, unable to engross herself in any of the books she had brought. That was a first, particularly since she had only just begun a new novel by Mrs. Radcliffe that promised to be most intriguing. Yet instead of concentrating upon the tale, she found herself thinking about her betrothed. Worse, her every thought was tinged with sentimentality.

She took out her pen and ink to work upon her own book, but the story evaded her completely. It seemed flat and disinteresting compared to her current situation. Instead, she sought to make sense of her intended on paper. In the bottom of her valise was a collection of calling cards she had appropriated when last at the duke's London house. They were useful as bookmarks and for scribbling notes. She chose one from Mme. de Roye, as the lady in question was a clear-thinking individual. It could not hurt to have a measure of her former governess' influence in this matter.

Eurydice drew a line to divide the back of the card into columns, then a plus sign above one and a minus above the other. The positive side was too easy to fill. Sebastian was handsome, charming, titled and rich enough for her. He had a mischievous sense of humor and could make her laugh. He was not witless, by any means. He possessed both a house in town and one in the country, both with libraries. She pursed her lips, tapped the pen, then added another trait.

He could kiss very well.

She underlined 'very'.

Eurydice added that item to the list of his shortcomings as well. He could only kiss well because he had a great deal of experience with that particular feat, because he was a rogue, a rake and a scoundrel. He consorted with many women and had seduced most of them, she would imagine. He had recounted his exploits since arriving at Airdfinnan, and Eurydice had never suspected a man would have such earthy appetites—while he complained of his dearth of companions. In London, he must bed a different woman every night.

There was every likelihood he had the French

disease already and their agreement might be moot in the end.

Eurydice looked out the window at the darkness, wondering why that prospect troubled her. They could annul the marriage for lack of consummation if no physician would assert his good health.

Could she believe any such assertion? Eurydice would not have put it past Sebastian to manufacture such a document to ensure that he had his way. She added 'untrustworthy' to the list on the negative side.

And that was the meat of the matter. She did not trust him—and worse, she did not trust herself in his presence, particularly when he touched her. It was all too easy to surrender to sensation—and Sebastian knew it. He tempted her on purpose.

He had no notion of what books were in his library. She underlined this fault, as well.

She added 'wicked' to Sebastian's list of faults, then amended it to 'mischievous'. She did not truly think there was any evil in him—he was simply 'selfish' with no regard for others.

He certainly would have expectations of a partner in bed, which compelled her to consider her own shortcomings. How on earth would she manage to keep his interest even for an interval every week? She knew virtually nothing about the pleasures of the flesh, even though she had studied the medical treatises in the duke's library.

Would he ruin her and abandon her? Or would he simply abandon her? Eurydice had no certainty of what Sebastian would do and that irked her. For example, just when she had braced herself to fend off his affections here at the inn, he had defended her with unexpected gallantry. He had ensured that she had a room of her own, a hot dinner, a firm bed and a key to lock the door herself. Evidently, it was not his scheme to ravish her before their vows were exchanged. Evidently, he could be relied upon to keep his word.

Or did he mean to lull her into complacency?

Eurydice could not say.

She wanted to trust Sebastian, but that trust would have to be earned more than it had been thus far.

Against every expectation, he believed in love and apparently had lost his heart once to no good end. That made her feel a bit sorry for him. How unexpected that he should be a romantic!

What if his beloved returned? If Eurydice was happily settled in the situation she desired, that prospect should not have mattered. To her horror, she discovered that it bothered her greatly.

He could not be succeeding in stealing her heart with such haste—could he?

Curse the man. She would be awake all the night thinking of him!

One of the books Eurydice had brought was a volume about the history of Britain and Scotland. She had chosen it in order to learn about Sebastian's own holding of Rockmorton, but now she opened it to refer to one of its excellent maps. She easily located Coldstream and could guess the location of this particular inn. It was a good day's ride eastward to the toll house, and could be done without entering Edinburgh.

Would she remain a maiden if she spent another day in the coach with Sebastian?

Eurydice could not be certain.

If she was not, and Sebastian did not wed her at Coldstream, then she would be a disgrace to her family. Eurydice was not so concerned about scandal for her own sake, but she didn't want to disappoint Daphne—especially as she would be reliant then upon the duke's support.

She went to bed, but remained awake, thoughts spinning with her uncertainty. No one had ever caused her a sleepless night and Eurydice had to wonder whether it was a good portent that she intended to wed the first individual to do so.

She was still awake when a gentle rain began to fall just before the dawn, and rose to wash and dress. She might have been the sole one out of bed when hoof beats clattered in the yard. Eurydice went to the window, curious as to who arrived so early in the day—and had therefore ridden all night—and her heart stopped cold.

It was the Duke of Inverfyre's coach that came to a halt in the yard. There was no mistaking either the vehicle or its familiar insignia. In the damp morning, the horses' breath turned to steam as they snorted and stamped. Alexander himself erupted from the carriage before it had halted completely, the storm on his countenance telling Eurydice more than she needed to know.

She hid herself instinctively, her breath coming quickly as she thought. Their scheme would be revealed and foiled, unless she made a quick choice. She summoned the maid to finish dressing, then flung her belongings into her valise. She wrote a note on the back of one of Sebastian's own calling cards before packing away her pen and swore the maid to secrecy with her last half-penny.

She could only hope that Sebastian understood and trusted her.

On the stairs to the kitchen, she encountered Jenkins, which surely was a sign that all would proceed in their favor. She gave him instructions and he hastened into the yard ahead of her. Eurydice's heart was hammering as she fled the inn, keeping to the shadows and out of view of the duke's driver.

Sebastian had been the one to advise her that she had to live an adventure in order to have a tale to tell. She was only taking the advice of her betrothed, after all.

Sebastian must have dozed for he was shaken awake with a jolt.

The light filtering into the tavern was pale silver, and he could hear a light rain falling on the roof. He felt chilled and his feet were downright cold. Someone had brought him a tankard of ale, leaving it upon the table before him.

More importantly, Armstrong leaned over him, shaking his shoulder as if he would wrench the bones loose. The duke looked tired, furious, and resolute. It was not an encouraging combination or Sebastian's favored way to greet the day.

"Where is she?" Armstrong demanded.

"Who?" Sebastian asked, though he knew exactly who his friend sought. Truly, the duke had shown more persistence than expected—or he had slept too long himself. How could he ensure that Eurydice was not discovered? He sat up, desperately trying to summon his wits.

"Eurydice, of course," Armstrong snapped, then glared at Sebastian. "Where *is* she?"

"How should I know such a thing?" It was Sebastian's favored ploy, to reply to a question with another one, particularly if that implied he did not know the answer. How intent was Armstrong upon locating her? The duke had ridden this far and at night, which indicated that he would not be readily swayed from the chase.

Sebastian pushed a hand through his hair when Armstrong relinquished his grip and felt the stubble on his chin. The chance of a good shave, let alone a hot bath, seemed remote in this moment.

The duke dropped into the chair opposite and studied him with narrowed eyes. Experience had proven that blue gaze could ferret out the most deeply buried secret, so Sebastian lifted his ale, the better to avoid that look, and took a sip.

What the deuce was he going to say?

Something fell from beneath the tankard and dropped in Sebastian's lap. Armstrong did not notice.

"She is gone," that man said. "Vanished from Airdfinnan the same time as you. Of course, I assumed she was with you, after what I witnessed just before your own departure."

Sebastian spared a glance down at the calling card, which was one of his own. How had it gotten beneath the tankard? To his surprise, there was writing on the other side.

Make haste!
—E

He blinked and read it again. The handwriting was almost, but not quite familiar. Eurydice had done a passing job of mimicking Esmeralda's hand. At another time, he might have admired the feat, but all he could think was that Eurydice was gone. She had left while he was sleeping, and as much as Sebastian wanted to pursue her immediately, he was keenly aware of Armstrong's watchful gaze.

To where should he make haste? Coldstream?

If she had left, had she taken his coach? His horse? Either could only put her in peril and he nearly leapt to his feet to ensure her safety.

"Do you know where she is?" Armstrong demanded.

Sebastian shook his head. Thanks to Eurydice's

choice, he had no notion where she might be found and he did not have to deceive his friend. Strangely enough, he did not feel a surge of gratitude toward his betrothed for this. "I have no idea."

It was true.

A maid brought a tankard of ale for the duke and he ignored it, leaning forward instead. "What is that you have?"

"A missive," he admitted, glad that Eurydice had used her wits.

The duke read it upside down and shook his head. "Your mistress pines for you, it appears."

"It does," Sebastian was content to let Armstrong believe it was from Esmeralda. How clever of Eurydice to have anticipated that the other man might see it.

"Did Eurydice confide in you, perhaps at dinner the other night?" the duke demanded. "You two were having a merry discussion."

"She was chiding me for reading so few books, and telling me of the wonders that might be found within your library." All true.

Armstrong's brows rose.

"She mentioned a medical treatise." Sebastian shrugged as if mystified, then drank more of his ale. At his gesture—which he contrived to make as leisurely as possible—the maid nodded that she would bring them fresh bread and cheese.

Where was Eurydice? Sebastian felt he'd been given a puzzle to solve without enough clues—or sufficient sleep.

"Why are you on this road then?" It seemed that Armstrong would not be easily waylaid.

But then, he had ridden all this way.

Sebastian conjured an explanation. "If you must know, I met a lady from Edinburgh last summer who insisted that I should call when in the vicinity." This was unassailably true. He smiled. "I contrive to be in her vicinity."

Armstrong's smile was reluctant. He sat back, though, and sipped of his ale, glancing at the card, then studying Sebastian closely. "What of Miss Ballantyne?"

"She need never know." Sebastian realized he had never replied to Esmeralda's missive. He still had Eurydice's version in his pocket but no additional paper at the ready. What if he sent that to Esmeralda? Would she know the difference?

"Doubtless she will be thrilled."

"I have no such expectation," Sebastian said. "I have been away a long while."

Armstrong nodded at the card. "And you ignored her injunction."

"Indeed." Sebastian did not like misleading his friend, but he knew Eurydice had been right about the duke's power to end their match. That man had a concern for her welfare that was good if inconvenient.

Sebastian was concerned for her welfare himself, though he knew how and why she had left the duke's holding. Why had she left *him*? Where had she gone?

"I thought you two might have contrived an escape together." Armstrong punctuated this with a glare. "I was thinking you might ride to Gretna Green," he added, as watchful as one of his hunting hawks.

Sebastian snorted, trying to dismiss the suggestion. In point of fact, it was troubling to be so readily anticipated. "But then I would be wed! Can you truly imagine that I would willingly enter the parson's mousetrap? Much less that I would do as much with an innocent maiden? You know me too well to believe such a possibility!"

It was not quite a lie, for Sebastian had not denied the idea outright—he had simply expressed skepticism that Armstrong might believe such a story.

Armstrong did not take as readily to the ploy as Sebastian might have hoped. He set aside his ale and spoke with grim resolve. "Know that I will go through every chamber in this place before I depart. If I find her and you are deceiving me, Montgomery, we shall duel."

Sebastian swallowed, though he contrived to hide his concern. The simple fact was that Alexander was a far better shot than he. A duel between them was not likely to end in his favor. As vexed as Armstrong was, he would not waste his shot.

Relief came from the most unlikely of corners, for Jenkins cleared his throat to reveal his presence. "All is ready, as you instructed, sir," he said after a bow. "We are prepared to leave at first light."

"Excellent," Sebastian said, leaving a coin for his ale. He gave no indication that he had not ordered the early departure and dared to hope that this was Eurydice's doing. He inclined his head to Armstrong. "You will excuse me, of course? I vowed to have luncheon in Edinburgh."

Armstrong frowned. "I will still search for her."

"And I wish you the best of luck."

Armstrong's eyes narrowed to blue slits, but Sebastian took his leave while he could. He was in the yard before he addressed Jenkins in an undertone, unable to quell his concern. "Is she...?"

Jenkins nodded. "I hope I was right to take instruction, my lord."

"Indeed, you were."

Sebastian's coach was waiting, his driver looking sleepy but prepared to depart all the same. Jenkins held the door and Sebastian swept into the coach, hiding his relief that Eurydice was tucked into a corner, clutching that umbrella. The surge of relief that passed through him was almost overwhelming in its intensity. If anything had happened to her...

It was not just Armstrong's retaliation he feared, to be sure.

"Were you seen?" he asked quietly, smiling as he waved toward Armstrong, who stood watching from the doorway to the inn.

"I should never have gotten this far if I had been," she replied quite reasonably.

Sebastian rapped on the roof, then treated

himself to a pinch of snuff, as if he had not a care in the world. The coach turned and left the yard, but he did not breathe a sigh of relief until the inn was far behind them.

That had been too close for comfort.

CHAPTER FOUR

Y ou are quiet," Eurydice said when they had traveled a goodly distance in silence. She had never known Sebastian to be content with the company of his own thoughts, but he had not spoken since they left the inn. "Are you vexed with me?"

"I am considering the potential risk to my person resulting from this match," he said, then granted her a grim look. "Armstrong means to challenge me to a duel if I am found to have any involvement in your disappearance from Airdfinnan."

"I suppose we should have anticipated as much," she said, wondering at his concern.

"For one who is not yet wed, you are quick to embrace the prospect of widowhood."

Eurydice laughed, thinking he made a jest, but he

did not even smile. She frowned then. "Surely you do not think he will catch us?"

"I cannot see how he will not."

"But surely you will not lose?"

"Surely I will. Armstrong is an infinitely better shot than I am. It comes from consistently shooting things."

"That cannot be. You came to Airdfinnan for the hunting..."

He interrupted her crisply. "And who fells more birds than I do, each and every time?"

Eurydice blinked. "I thought you were not trying."

"I assure you that my efforts make no difference." Sebastian shook a finger at her. "And he will not waste a shot. He is furious."

Eurydice was not certain of the import of this, so she asked. "Do you change your mind as a result?"

"No, but we must change the terms of our agreement," he said immediately and with such resolve that she knew there would be no negotiation. "He intends to search the inn for you, and he will not find you. He will conclude that you were in my coach, and he will follow us."

"He cannot keep us from wedding!"

"Of course, he can. But if we are committed to this course, then we must be equally committed to the match."

"What does that mean?"

Sebastian shot her an intense look that launched

a shiver through her. "That it will be consummated immediately. This very night. It is our sole chance to eliminate his objections."

"But..." Eurydice felt hot and then she felt cold. "But the French disease..."

Sebastian shook his head. "You will have to accept my word with regards to my good health."

"But thirty days..."

"You will have to write your book *after* we have conceived. We will remain in London until that happy news, then you can retreat to Cornwall, write your book and deliver our son."

She had never seen Sebastian so resolute. His eyes glinted and his lips were set.

He leaned closer and dropped his voice low. The carriage suddenly seemed very small. "I do not mean to die just yet, Eurydice. So, you must choose. Either you agree to these new terms or I will surrender you to Armstrong myself with all haste."

Eurydice was horrified. "You cannot!"

"I will," he said, and she could not be certain whether it was merely a dare or not. "I doubt he is an hour behind us. We can see you en route to Airdfinnan before luncheon."

"You would not." Eurydice feared, though, that he would.

"To save my own hide, I most certainly would," Sebastian replied with surety. "If you know nothing of me, you must know that."

She sat back, thoughts churning. She did not want to return to Airdfinnan and she did want to marry Sebastian. She liked him more with each passing exchange and was even more convinced of the merit of their match.

Never mind that her curiosity was awakened about the intimacies exchanged between man and wife. If she agreed, this very night she would *know*. The prospect stole her breath away, but not her wits. If their match was consummated, then it could not be annulled. Her financial future would be secure.

And against every expectation, she trusted Sebastian in this. Was it the change in his manner, or the fact that his heart had once been wounded? Eurydice could not say, but she was utterly certain.

She trusted in that, as well.

"I agree," she said, offering her hand.

Sebastian's good mood was immediately restored. He smiled and his eyes twinkled as he folded his hand around hers. "I do so admire that you have good sense," he murmured, his words so low and silky that she shivered.

"You knew I would accept your terms," she charged.

"I gambled that you would, and it appears I was right." He grinned at her. "Could it be that you are not so immune to my charm, after all?"

"Perhaps my choices are limited."

"There is always choice, Eurydice," he said softly, then gave her hand a little tug, pulling her closer. "Fear not, Eurydice, I will ensure the first time is as good as it can be."

And before she could dispute that assertion, Sebastian kissed her again. The kiss was different than his earlier two, for it was more leisurely and cajoling. How could there be so many kinds of kisses? Eurydice knew she would have to begin a list.

Then, because he had contrived to win her agreement, she felt compelled to be less predictable. Eurydice kissed him back, suspecting that she had to meet him halfway to persuade him of her own conviction. She twined her fingers into his hair and met his ardor with a measure of her own.

Sebastian caught his breath as if surprised, then pulled her into his lap, slanting his mouth over hers and kissing her more deeply. The sensation was remarkably pleasurable, launching shivers over her flesh and awakening a heat in her belly. Eurydice found herself enjoying this kiss far more than she had ever thought possible. She opened her mouth to him, touching her tongue boldly to his, and Sebastian made an incoherent sound that thrilled her.

Was it possible that she had some power in this transaction?

Was it possible that Sebastian found her alluring?

Or had he simply been too long without an intimate union?

Eurydice cared less than she knew she should. She wrapped her arms around his neck, savoring the hard strength of him against her. His hands slid down her back in a smooth caress that made her heart skip and he twined one of her curls around his finger before stroking her cheek.

He was gentle as well as passionate and Eurydice was reassured.

All too soon Sebastian broke his kiss and settled her on the seat beside him. He cleared his throat and looked out the window, as if they were perfect strangers. But Eurydice saw the flick of pulse at his throat and the way he clenched his hand. They were both equally affected by that embrace and she could think of no better sign for their scheme of conception.

Surely a practical match could have its pleasures?

All the same, she had no notion what to say, a rare and awkward situation. The carriage bounced onward, the horses galloped and the whip snapped. The rain drummed on the roof and the windows were steamed so that the view was obscured. Eurydice's pulse gradually slowed and her breath steadied. Her lips continued to burn, though, and that delicious tingle did not subside. Sebastian's thigh was so close to her own that she could feel the heat emanating from him.

And most curious of all, she had no care for her books.

If this was but a kiss, she clearly had need of further information to prepare herself for the night ahead. She untied her bundle of books and selected the medical treatise from the duke's library. She took a fortifying breath, then opened it to a chapter she had never yet dared to read.

But before she had turned the third page, her sleepless night and the rhythm of the coach caught up with her. Eurydice's eyelids drooped and the book slid from her grasp as she fell asleep, her head on Sebastian's shoulder.

❧

Sebastian caught the book as it slipped from Eurydice's lap but had to read the title of the selected chapter twice.

Coitus.

Then he read the first paragraph to verify that the subject was as expected.

He closed the book and smiled. She actually had brought the medical treatise and was consulting it with regards to their wedding night ahead. Sebastian chuckled and tucked the book into the bundle with the others. He tucked his cloak around his betrothed and drew her against his side, watching her sleep. She had been awake early enough to witness the duke's arrival. She slept so deeply now that he wondered whether she had slept at all the night before.

What did she know of intimacies between man and wife? Likely very little. Her mother had died when she was a small child and Sebastian could not imagine Lady Octavia enlightening her granddaughters. Did Eurydice talk about private matters with her sister, the duchess? Possibly, but if that were the case, whatever she had learned had been insufficient to satisfy her curiosity.

Hence the book.

He would have to take great care this night to ensure that she had her pleasure. She learned quickly, that was for certain, for already she showed an alacrity with kissing that tempted him to forget her innocence. He sighed, knowing that restraint was not one of his better traits.

But there had been a chance to end their arrangement, and Eurydice had not taken it. Not only had she ensured their escape, but she had accepted the change of terms. The notion that she truly did wish to wed him gave Sebastian a warm glow about his heart. Perhaps she too felt something dawning between them. Could it be that people found a love match like that of his parents in other ways? He knew his father had been smitten at first glance, and perhaps, if he met Eurydice now for the first time, Sebastian's reaction might be the same. It was not all bad that they had known each other for years, for that fostered a trust between them that could not be quickly gained. He looked down at her and touched one of those errant curls, knowing that he would miss her pert commentary when she departed for his country house.

In fact, he came to suspect that London might have less appeal without the prospect of Eurydice's company. He thought about introducing her to the pleasures of the city and knew he would spoil her dreadfully at the dressmakers and other shops. He knew she had been to the theatre, but he would take her to all manner of exhibitions and shows. He would teach her to drive his carriage, just to see her eyes light with triumph, and he would indulge her in bookstores, just to make her smile. He fully expected that she would not allow him to evade his responsibilities and he did not mind that in the least.

Would their son favor her or him? He hoped the boy was fair with Eurydice's eyes. He hoped the boy had her wits. He hoped, rather wickedly, that they might have a girl—or several—first.

What of her book? What kind of story was she writing? Would she let him read it? He found himself cursedly curious as to its subject, and a little jealous that it had such a hold over her imagination. She would even wed him to guarantee her writing time. Perhaps she would trust him with an excerpt in time.

Sebastian was so snared by his musings that it seemed they reached the tollhouse quickly. In truth, it was after luncheon, but he did not find himself hungry at all. He was too concerned about bringing their plan to fruition. He awakened Eurydice and escorted her from the carriage.

The service itself was short and unembellished, a bit disappointing, to be sure. There were no flowers, no music, no friends and family gathered to witness the event. The tollhouse was built of stone and illuminated by a single lantern, which was not nearly sufficient to make it merry on such a dreary day. The rain pounded down unceasingly. The officiant droned through the words as if he read a list for the market, but Eurydice smiled up at Sebastian, her eyes alight in the most alluring way. She repeated her vows without hesitation, her hands clasped within his, and when he said his part, the deed was done.

He paid the fee and took Eurydice's hand, knowing that half of London would be astonished to find him married. "And now to Edinburgh," he said to Eurydice with a smile that she returned. When they reached the carriage, Jenkins held the door, then offered his congratulations. Sebastian thanked him then dropped his voice low. "Bamburgh will be our destination, if you please. There is a large inn there, if I remember correctly."

"Of course, my lord."

"You think His Grace will follow us here and thence onward," Eurydice said softly when they were underway again.

"Why should he not?"

She nodded thoughtfully. "How far is Bamburgh?"

"We will arrive before dinner, eat in our rooms, then see the deed done. It is possible we will be found this very evening."

Eurydice bit her lip. "I will write to Daphne in the morning, before we depart," she said. "I cannot leave her to worry."

"And by then, our match will be fixed." He took her hand. "You remain certain?"

"I do."

"I found the service uninspired. You?"

"It was efficient," she acknowledged with a

quick sidelong smile and he laughed.

"I would have liked there to have been flowers."

"Then let us fill your house with them once in London."

"Our house, Eurydice," he said, kissing her fingertips. "It will be your home, as well."

Her eyes sparkled. "My library, perhaps, in your house," she teased. "I cannot wait to inventory your books." She reached for her own but he stopped her with a touch.

"Leave that wretched volume alone. I will show you all you need to know of coitus."

She flushed crimson. "But I like to be prepared..."

"I assure you, all will be well." He brushed his lips across hers once again, hearing her catch her breath and knew it would be so.

He would ensure as much.

"Now, tell me of your book."

"I..."

"Some shred of detail, Eurydice, as a token of your trust." He thought she might not take the dare but he should have known better.

She settled against him and began to talk softly, and Sebastian knew a curious satisfaction that was all new.

It seemed that Eurydice was not the sole one encountering new experiences.

The inn was lovely, well-appointed and

comfortable, and their rooms were large and gracious. There was both a sitting room and the bedroom, with its great carved oaken bed. The maid bustled around, lighting fires in both rooms, turning down the bed, setting a table for supper in the sitting room. Lamps cast a welcome golden light in both rooms. Eurydice suspected that the sitting room had a fine view of the sea, but on this night, the rain obscured it—and then the maid drew the drapes over the window, as well, to preserve the heat. Even the sound of the rain was muffled.

The meal was hearty fare, plentiful and blessedly hot. By the time they had eaten their fill, she felt nearly herself again. She had been a little shy about telling Sebastian anything of her book, but he was an attentive listener and asked sensible questions. He had taken her endeavor seriously, which was unexpected—and very nice. Indeed, she had a short list of considerations about the direction of her story, thanks to his inquiries.

How curious that she was not in the least bit interested in them on this night.

Sebastian stood after the meal, and said he would retire to the common room for a cup of ale. She understood that he meant to watch for the duke. In the meantime, two maids brought a bath for Eurydice and filled it in the sitting room. She was relieved to remove her mired clothes and to sink into the wondrous warmth of the water. One maid vowed to launder her undergarments by the morning, seeing as Eurydice had packed so lightly.

On another night, she might have savored her bath and the prospect of reading in the cozy rooms, but she knew what was ahead. She did not dread their inevitable intimacy, not precisely, but she never liked being unprepared. Eurydice did not linger, but rose from the tub while the water was still warm, not waiting for the maid's return. She donned her chemise and combed out her hair, noting that her hand shook slightly. She retreated into the bedroom as Sebastian and Jenkins returned, closing the door almost completely.

She could not resist the allure of that medical treatise, though she was unable to concentrate on the words as she heard Sebastian disrobe. She opened the book to the same page and tried to read, sitting on the one chair in the room. Sebastian shared a jest or two with Jenkins, then she heard the water splash as he bathed, as well. He was not shy about taking his bath and truly, she was reminded of the enthusiasm of birds for puddles in the garden. She yearned to peek, but kept her gaze fixed on the book, well aware that Jenkins was yet in the sitting room. The water splashed finally and Sebastian thanked the servants who came to take the tub away. He bade Jenkins a goodnight, then the door to the corridor was shut.

Eurydice heard a key turn in the lock and then there was silence.

Her mouth went dry and she ran a fingertip down the page, not comprehending the words at all. It was so quiet that she could not be certain of

Sebastian's location, if he had moved at all. The hair pricked on the back of her neck, as if she was being watched, and her heart skipped a beat.

"Are there illustrations in that chapter?" he murmured from startling proximity.

Eurydice jumped and dared to look. He was standing in the doorway in a silk robe, arms folded across his chest, dark gaze fixed upon her. He looked larger and more dangerous than he had earlier, as well as quite unpredictable. His hair was wet, but those dark eyes seemed to pierce all her secrets. He did not even appear to blink.

Had she ever seen a more handsome man?

Eurydice swallowed. "Very few." His silk robe was loosely belted but hung open to his waist. It was gold with a rich sheen, but almost the same hue as the tanned skin of his forearms. She could see his bare chest, graced with dark curly hair, and a great many intriguing shadows. She did not dare to let her gaze drop lower.

Sebastian nodded solemnly, even as a twinkle lit in those eyes. "How vexing to have so little information on a matter of such great concern."

"Indeed," she agreed, feeling that the room was unnaturally warm.

He took a step into the room and dominated the space, filling it with his presence and his warmth. Eurydice was not certain she could take a full breath.

"Perhaps this is a circumstance in which experience is better than the knowledge gained from books," he suggested.

"Perhaps," she managed to agree.

He looked pointedly at the book. Eurydice set it aside, heart hammering. He beckoned to her with one strong hand and she rose to her feet, hating that her knees trembled. Sebastian moved closer, his ease with the situation completely at odds with her uncertainty. His hands fell to the belt of his robe and Eurydice looked down, noting that his feet were bare on the carpet. "What do you most want to know?" he asked softly and again, she was aware of the patter of the rain, the crackle of the fire.

She took a steadying breath. "I would like to see," she confessed. "I cannot envision how..."

"You must have your examination of my person," he teased. He laughed when she blushed, unfastened the belt, then shrugged out of the robe. It fell to the carpet in a puddle of golden silk as he lifted his hands.

Eurydice stared. His body was more different from her own than she could have imagined it might be. He was all hard planes and smooth surfaces, taut with muscled strength, spare and lean. He was beautiful, elegantly proportioned and powerful. He was also vigorously healthy and unblemished. He turned, his hands raised, letting her survey him completely. When he faced her again, she realized he was smiling at her.

He was also clearly aroused.

"It is not always thus," she said. "It could not be."

"It is not," he agreed. "Anticipation changes its state as does arousal, of course."

"How very curious." She leaned closer for a better look and he laughed again.

"It is no different from your own body, in some ways."

"Your body is very different from mine."

"But not in showing the effects of arousal."

"I do not understand."

He gestured to her chemise with a playful fingertip. "Your turn."

A lump rose in Eurydice's throat. She did not think she was particularly lovely and feared suddenly that he would find her charms inadequate. "You cannot look upon me."

"Of course, I can and I will. We are wed, Eurydice." His tone left no room for negotiation.

"But you might not like me."

He looked down at his erection, then lifted his gaze to hers. That twinkle was back. "I assure you that I do."

She laughed then, surprised into it, and his own smile spread wider.

Eurydice reached for the tie of her chemise, but her fingers fumbled with the simple bow. Sebastian closed the distance between them and lifted her hands away. He planted a kiss on each palm, his gaze flicking to hers, before he untied the bow slowly himself.

"There is nothing to fear," he murmured softly, opening the neck of her chemise with his fingertips, sliding them across her shoulders.

His touch left a warm trail across her skin. She stood, holding his gaze, and waited.

"Your body also shows its arousal," he whispered, easing the garment from one shoulder. Her breast was exposed and she glanced down to find the nipple taut.

"See?" Sebastian slid his hand lower, cupping the weight of her breast, then eased his thumb over that tight peak.

Eurydice caught her breath at the jolt that raced through her body.

"And look again," he advised.

She saw that it was even tighter and more ruddy. Her throat tightened and she felt warm beyond all.

He winked at her, the very image of mischief, then bent his head and kissed her nipple.

No, he suckled it and the sensation was a marvel.

Eurydice caught her breath, then found herself clutching his shoulder as the pleasure rolled through her body. His skin was smooth and warm, and she felt his muscled power. When he released the nipple, it was even more turgid and red.

"I did not know," she confessed in a whisper, but Sebastian gave his attention to the other.

She reached out, feeling bold, and touched one of his nipples. It was flatter than hers, but the peak rose to her touch in the same way. She bent on impulse and kissed it, then suckled it as he had done with hers, and heard him catch his breath.

"Minx," he whispered and she laughed.

"It *is* similar," she said.

"And here," he said, guiding her hand to his erection. She touched him, timidly at first but then with increasing confidence as he guided her. There was a bead of moisture on the tip. He reached between her thighs and Eurydice gasped when she felt his caress. His fingertip, too, glistened with moisture when he showed it to her.

"Why?" she whispered.

"That is different. Your moisture facilitates our union, and mine is the precursor of the result of our union."

"The semen is released..."

He touched her lips with his other hand. "If you recite from that book, we will never proceed," he warned and she smiled a little.

"It seems incredible," she said, eying the size of him.

"It feels incredible."

She flicked a look at him, thinking he might be jesting with her but he was deadly serious. "I thought it would hurt."

"Maybe not as much as you anticipate. I will do my best," he vowed, and then, before Eurydice could ask, Sebastian lifted her in his arms, kissing her to silence in the same smooth gesture. She felt that she was floating, then he placed her on the bed, still kissing her as his fingertips feathered over her body.

She kept her eyes closed, concentrating on his touch and how her body awakened to his caress. His hand moved between her thighs and she gasped when he touched her, astonished by the pleasure he conjured with his touch.

It was not long before she felt a tumult building within her, something she had never experienced before but which felt exactly right just the same—though not as right as the release that left her trembling in its wake.

That truly shook every last one of her assumptions about matrimony and the merit of having a spouse.

Eurydice was a marvel and Sebastian knew himself to be lost.

She was both shy and bold, willing to experience a new sensation but uncertain how to proceed. She learned quickly, though, mimicking Sebastian's movements with such alacrity that his resolve to take it slow was almost overwhelmed. She gained her release with astonishing speed, for she was remarkably responsive, and he found himself beguiled by her delighted smile and the rosy flush that tinted her skin. It was clearly her first and he felt a sense of triumph that she was so delighted.

How unexpected that he, who was no stranger to amorous liaisons, should feel on the brink of a new discovery just as Eurydice was. Her sense of wonder made him appreciate the marvel of a happy union—and ensured that he wished to make all of this wondrous for her.

He had to be leisurely.

Sebastian stretched out beside her and kissed her then, coaxing her ardor again with his caresses. He felt as if they were sheltered in a haven of warmth and golden light, safe from the world and its woes—even as he was aware that Armstrong had to be coming ever closer. He caressed her again, watching her arch to his touch, then she stroked him with newfound confidence.

"That cannot be all," she whispered in a husky voice, her eyes dancing. "You have not had such release."

Sebastian rolled to his back, encouraging her to straddle him. It would be easier for her atop him. Eurydice surveyed him with a satisfaction that made him smile, and he could not resist the golden splendor of the curls tumbling to her waist. Her hair was a marvel, tumbles of golden curls that belonged in a Renaissance painting.

"I have you at my mercy," she teased.

"You do, indeed," he confessed, for it was true. He was in thrall to her and he was not surprised that she guessed as much.

Her gaze fell upon his erection again, then she sobered and met his gaze once more. "I do not know what to do." She wrinkled her nose in that most adorable fashion but did not retreat. "Show me," she invited in a whisper that resonated in his veins.

His daring bride. Sebastian guided her to rise above him, then eased himself against her. She was so soft and welcoming that he caught his breath, then moved against her slowly.

"Oh!" Eurydice whispered, exhaling the sound, then she eased herself lower. He whispered to her, advising her to be slow and gentle, knowing that she might kill him before she had explored him to her satisfaction. She ran her hands across his chest and closed her eyes as she took all of him, then laid her cheek against his chest.

"Oh," she said again, a strain in her voice, and he felt her tremble. His arms were full of her soft sweetness, and her hair tangled around his fingers, spilling onto his chest. He kissed her temple, then moved within her, hearing her gasp again. She sat up and braced her hands against him, her eyes shining and her cheeks flushed. She moved then of her own volition, and it was Sebastian who was overwhelmed with pleasure.

"Temptress," he managed to whisper. "I intended to teach you!"

Eurydice laughed and moved again, watching him closely as she learned what he liked best. Her pride in her ability to please him might have been the most seductive thing he had ever seen. Sebastian was lost in a haze of pleasure, captive to his new wife's determination to satisfy him. She moved and she halted, she caressed him and she kissed him, she rode him with increasing confidence until he thought he might not live to see the morn.

Eurydice rocked atop him with increasing confidence and Sebastian could not decide whether he wanted her to take him to the summit or continue her sweet torment all the night long. Time stopped and the candlelight flickered, the room filled with a glow that was theirs alone. She moved with increasing vigor and his pulse thundered with rising need. His heart was pounding and his chest was tight, his very skin seemed to be stretched taut yet he hoped to last until she found her pleasure again.

Then she reached back and caressed him on the underside of his scrotum.

Sebastian roared with the fullness of his release, gripping her hips and driving deep until he could conjure no more.

When he was trembling in the wake of his release, Eurydice tumbled to the bed beside him. He did not have to look to know that her eyes were dancing with satisfaction. He was too busy catching his breath.

And this had been only the first time.

"Wherever did you learn that?" he demanded when he could speak.

"It is in the book," she confessed, and he turned in time to see her smile at his obvious surprise. She was glorious, her hair a-tangle, gilded from the candlelight, her eyes shining and he could only stare in wonder. It was how he had envisioned her, aglow in the wake of pleasure, gorgeous and alluring.

How had she made this feat entirely new?

It was love that changed all and Sebastian knew it well.

"Many men have an area of sensitivity beneath the scrotum, which, if pressed or caressed before ejaculation vastly increases the pleasure of that deed." Eurydice explained, obviously quoting the relevant passage.

"Forget what I said about not needing the book," Sebastian growled and she laughed with a delight that prompted his own smile.

He had already reached for the cloth to wash up when he saw the blood on the linens. The sight made him realize that all had changed. Eurydice was his wife and always would be. There could be no annulment.

The match with Eurydice had been like a jest, and Sebastian had agreed with the surety that he risked nothing at all. Now his heart clenched, for he had stepped directly into the one situation he had sworn to avoid forever.

He was falling in love with his wife, and she did not believe in love. He flicked a glance her way to find her frowning slightly as she checked the book for more suggestions. She had experienced pleasure, to be sure, but sensation had not awakened emotion.

He would be a stud and a source of financial security to her and no more.

How would he bear it?

Sebastian had to leave this chamber and consider his path, before he was seduced by his bride again.

What was amiss?

Eurydice had been certain that all was well, then Sebastian's manner had abruptly changed. He had become still and his expression had turned inscrutable. It had been the blood on the linens that had prompted the change, though she could not say why. He had known she was a maiden. Did he regret that they were thoroughly wed, and that it was too late for an annulment? He had dressed quickly and left her, ignoring her questions and calls, even though it was the middle of the night.

As the moments passed and he did not return, Eurydice feared that he found her company disappointing.

She had seen Esmeralda Ballantyne once, at the theater, and readily recalled that woman's beauty and poise in his moment of doubt. Miss Ballantyne was elegant and assured, perfectly attired, and as different from Eurydice as it was possible to be. Eurydice knew she would not benefit from a comparison.

Sebastian had regrets.

Eurydice washed and donned her chemise, then sat on the edge of the bed, trying to identify precisely what had gone awry. She must have failed to satisfy him. Was there some art to ensuring a man's pleasure that she did not know? Eurydice expected that there was and that she had failed some secret test, but even a vigorous study of the medical volume did not reveal any helpful detail.

Indeed, after this interval, she could have written

a more compelling description of coitus than the book contained.

Previously, she had admired how Sebastian did not hold back in expressing his views or revealing his thoughts. She had found him easy company, but evidently those who met him abed saw another side of his nature. Would he be moody like this each week when they met abed? The book offered no suggestions that a person's manner might change after intimate knowledge of another.

Eurydice could only conclude that their mating had fallen short of his expectations.

But if he did not confide in her or explain the trouble, how could she do better?

Why would he not confide in her?

Eurydice was mystified and no amount of pondering her husband's actions that night proved to be illuminating at all.

When he returned, it was almost dawn. Eurydice feigned sleep, for she did not know what to say. He undressed in darkness and laid down with his back toward her. While she tried to choose the best words to utter first, she heard his breathing slow.

In moments, she knew he was soundly asleep, and her questions would have to wait. She would have neither answers nor sleep this night.

What an inconvenient man he was.

CHAPTER FIVE

On the morning after her wedding, Eurydice awakened early. On this day, though, instead of writing or reading, she remained in bed and watched Sebastian sleep. He looked younger in slumber, his hair tousled and his breathing slow. She felt the most curious sensation in the region of her heart, gratitude mixed with yet more, for he had been a gentle yet passionate lover. He had ensured her pleasure first and been patient with her ignorance, and it had seemed to her that something marvelous had dawned between them. It felt tentative and precious, as fragile as a butterfly—and in truth, it had been dismissed all too quickly.

She had to repair the matter, somehow.

Eurydice studied Sebastian and wished she could read his thoughts and divine his secrets. She was not sufficiently bold to awaken him with a touch, so convinced was she that she had erred the night before.

She had to make matters right somehow.

The sky had turned pearly when she heard the hoof beats. She guessed who arrived outside the inn, by the speed of the horses. She went to the bedroom window and looked all the same. The duke appeared to be more tired, but the glance he fired up at the inn was so fiercely blue that Eurydice took a step back.

Her heart stopped cold.

She could not let him challenge Sebastian to a duel.

She had to resolve the situation favorably, for she was not prepared to surrender her new husband yet—no matter how incomprehensible he might be. Eurydice did not doubt that the two friends might argue if they confronted each other and she had to hope that she had more skill with diplomacy than she was rumored to possess.

When the maid came to say that a gentleman called for the earl, Eurydice was half-dressed. She dressed quickly with the girl's assistance, then left Sebastian sleeping when she went down to meet the duke.

He was pacing in the common room, and spun to confront her. "I knew it," he said through his teeth, then took a step closer, those eyes flashing. "Is Montgomery too cowardly to show his face?"

"Of course not," Eurydice said, speaking crisply. She had noted before that the duke responded to such shows of confidence. "He is sound asleep."

"I will not speculate upon the reason for that," the duke muttered darkly.

"Will you break your fast with me?" Eurydice smiled. "I suppose it is too much to hope that you have a London newspaper? I do so enjoy it in the morning."

The duke exhaled in frustration, then surveyed her. "It is done, then?"

"It is done and I am content." She gestured to a table, well aware that the maid listened avidly.

"You should not have done it."

She kept her tone reasonable. "But you would never have allowed it if I had asked you."

"He will not make you happy, Eurydice," the duke warned in a low growl. "The heart is no good guide in these matters when it comes to some men..."

"I did not wed for love, Your Grace," Eurydice said, boldly interrupting him. He fell silent and stared at her. "I said once that I would wed a rogue, that he might do as he desired in town and I might retreat to his country house to write."

"But that was just a girlish whimsy."

"On the contrary, I still believe it to be a sensible course. I do not mean to change Sebastian's ways, and I have no expectations of doing so." Even as she spoke, Eurydice realized that her expectations had changed. She did not want to retreat to Cornwall, not if it meant leaving Sebastian behind in London. "Our agreement is that I will give him a son and he will grant me the freedom I desire. It is blessedly simple."

The duke sat down heavily. "I cannot imagine this will prove sufficient for you."

"It must, for I have chosen it, and you have saved the expense of giving me a season..."

"Which I would have spent gladly."

"And my sole regret is that you have pursued us so diligently and so far." Eurydice smiled again. "I appreciate, Your Grace, that you take great care of your responsibilities. I would have simply told you of my desire, but I did not believe you would agree."

"I would not have done so, for certain. Montgomery is not a suitable spouse for you."

"How can you speak thus of an old friend?"

The duke frowned. "He has changed since our younger days. He has come to care only for himself and the implications of that for you is my concern."

Eurydice was not convinced. Sebastian had been kind and considerate of her, even if he had been changeable the night before. She was confident that they would surmount whatever error she had made—if he deigned to speak to her again.

"Then we must contrive to dismiss your concerns," she said to the duke, knowing that neither he nor her sister would rest easy until they had seen her content with their own eyes. She had an idea about that. "We continue to London today and will remain there through the holiday season. Perhaps you might come for dinner on Christmas

Day? I am certain that Daphne would enjoy a visit to town."

The duke fought a smile and lost. "Christmas?" he said, then chuckled. "You must know that Montgomery despises the festive season."

Eurydice had no such idea. "Who can do as much?"

"I think you will learn much of your new husband in the coming weeks, Eurydice, and I shall be glad to witness the results." The duke nodded, accepting a tankard of ale and raising it to Eurydice. "I accept your invitation gladly, though I would give a shilling to see Montgomery's face when you share that news."

"But you are friends and he has just spent several months at Airdfinnan." Eurydice was dismissive of this concern, convinced as she was that the duke was unkind in his assessment of Sebastian.

"I look forward to the day. We will let you know when we arrive in town." The duke toasted her and drank deeply, more amused than Eurydice knew he should have been.

Sebastian did not truly despise Christmas, did he?

❧

"You did *what?*" Sebastian demanded of his new wife when he awakened just before midday. He had slept hard after fighting his doubts, but her confession brought him immediately to full consciousness.

Surely she made a jest!

But Eurydice was utterly serious. "I had to keep him from challenging you," she said, as if her invitation to the duke was an entirely reasonable solution. "You said yourself that you would lose, and I am not yet prepared to be without a spouse."

"I thank you for that," he said, more than a little annoyed by her tone. She could have made a sweet confession and reassured him completely, but Eurydice was maddeningly reasonable.

"We have a wager, sir." She lifted her hands. "You have not yet visited a solicitor to secure my future and who can say whether we have conceived your heir as yet? The book indicates..."

"Curse the book!" Sebastian roared, vexed beyond all.

At Christmas. Why had she been compelled to issue an invitation for Christmas? It was as if she would shred his heart before his very eyes. It was bad enough that he felt this magical sense of a dawning love, but she would make him confront what he had lost before he knew what he had gained. Sebastian felt in turmoil. He had planned to undertake the journey of conquering her reluctant heart in easy stages, but she leapt ahead without regard for his concerns.

A silent Eurydice watched him as warily as she might consider a rabid dog. "You are irked," she suggested cautiously.

"I am annoyed indeed!" Sebastian retorted. "You

have stepped far beyond your station, madame. I would never have invited the duke to my home during the season, and had you troubled to ask me, you would have known as much!" His voice rose over the course of this lecture but Eurydice was not daunted.

"You are not thinking clearly," she chided him gently. Sebastian bestowed his most chilling glare upon her, to no discernible effect. Indeed, she came closer. "You have just spent several happy months as the duke's guest at Airdfinnan. It is fitting to reciprocate. I asked them only for dinner!"

"Not at Christmas!"

She frowned and shook her head. "When else? My sister will not rest easy until she has witnessed our happy situation," she said, using a tone appropriate for soothing a wild beast. "The duke will not rest easy with my sister so unsettled and one meal..."

"I do not serve Christmas dinner in my home!" he repeated, biting off the words.

"Whyever not?"

"Because I do not celebrate Christmas."

"Of course, you do." Eurydice was dismissive. "You simply do not want to face him, but the sooner this is resolved, the better."

"I am no coward."

She lifted a brow. "Everyone has a festive dinner on Christmas, at the very least..."

"I do not. Not anymore."

"Then what do you eat on December 25th?"

"I usually drink." That was not entirely true. Sebastian had stopped drinking at any volume twelve years before. He cultivated a reputation of imbibing great quantities of wine and brandy, but in truth, he consumed very little.

He had been drunk when he had received the news. Never again.

Sebastian dropped into a chair, pushed a hand through his hair and tried to echo Eurydice's calm tone. He knew he failed. "This scheme is quite impossible and I would have told you as much if you had troubled to consult me. My servants know they have the day off, because they do each and every year. You must cancel this invitation and you must do so immediately."

Eurydice perched on the lip of a chair opposite. "And if I decline to do so?"

Her audacity confounded him. "Then you will have guests to dinner who find an empty table and no host."

She surveyed the room, obviously thinking. "And if I could contrive a meal without denying your servants their day of leisure?"

"You will not." Sebastian leaned forward so that they were almost nose to nose and held her gaze. "In fact, with this choice of yours, our plan must change again. You will depart immediately from London to Rockmorton Manor and remain there."

She looked startled, then inclined to argue with him. The gleam in her eyes was so remarkably stubborn that he dared to hope she did not wish to be parted from him, but her words dismissed that possibility. "But we have an agreement. How shall we conceive an heir then? How will I keep my side of our bargain?"

"Is this not what you desired initially?" Sebastian countered. "You will have the run of the house, and I will stay in town, and you may feed Christmas dinner in Cornwall to whoever you like! Perhaps you will even discover that you are with child and can send me the happy news."

She fixed him with a look. "You are afraid."

"I assure you I am not." It was a lie and Sebastian hoped she did not know it.

"Liar," she said flatly, proving his worst fear true. She could see the secrets of his very heart. They had to part ways. "Why do you refuse to celebrate Christmas?"

"I will not speak of it."

A familiar glint lit Eurydice's eyes and he knew before she spoke that she would not follow his instruction. "Tell me why and I will consider cancelling my invitation."

"You will cancel it either way. You will *not* be in town."

She folded her arms across her chest. "This is about last night, is it not? I disappointed you in my...actions."

Sebastian was astonished that she could think he would find fault with their glorious union. It had been transformative, magical, a prospect of future joy...but she had not seen it that way. There could be no more compelling evidence that he alone was emotionally entangled in this match.

Eurydice shook her head, not waiting for him to continue. "No one performs any act perfectly on the first occasion for it. I would ask you for instruction that I might improve for the next time..."

She would wear him down. She would steal his heart, and then she would lock herself in his library, ignoring him forevermore once she had her security, and he would be bereft again.

Not again.

Sebastian could not bear the possibility.

"There will be no next time!" he insisted.

She regarded him as if he had lost his wits. "You have great confidence in the power of a single union to produce a child. The book..."

"—is of no merit whatsoever," he said, interrupting her crisply. "You will leave London for Cornwall and there will be no second incident and we will speak of this no more." He took a breath, uncertain why precisely he did not feel in command of this situation, even though he was making plenty of commands. "And you will cancel your invitation." He turned to the washstand, resisting the urge to dunk his head into the cold water. That might clear his thoughts.

"No, I will not cancel it," she repeated. "You will not deny me the pleasure of Christmas with my sister and her children, whether you choose to celebrate the season or not."

"Go to Cornwall then!"

"And how shall we conceive your heir at such distance?"

"Perhaps I will visit, in the spring."

She lifted a brow. "And how many mistresses will you have bedded during the interval? No, sir, we must conceive that son first, before you resume your ways, which means I must remain in town."

He pivoted to face her, hoping his expression was daunting. "Did you not pledge to obey me just yesterday afternoon?" he demanded.

Eurydice smiled but her eyes narrowed and her posture was taut. "You could not have expected that concession to be so readily won, particularly when you are irrational, sir."

"Irrational?" The charge stung because Sebastian knew it was true.

If she had pledged a dawning affection then his resistance would have been overwhelmed, if she had wept a single tear, he would have been undone, but Eurydice, being Eurydice, argued with a cold logic that only fed his dread of the future.

"You need a son. We are wed. I will remain in town until I conceive, which certainly will not be by Christmas, and even if it is, no physician will be certain in so few weeks." She took a breath. "And in the meantime, my invitation will ensure that you are not shot in a duel."

Sebastian had to respect that she did not back down readily.

He heartily disliked that she was not ceding to

his will. "Eurydice..." he began, his voice a low growl.

She stood and brushed her skirts with purpose. "What do you drink Christmas day?"

"Brandy." It was a lie but one she would believe.

"Then I will ensure you have sufficient when I provision for our guests." She turned to leave their chamber, her manner so satisfied that Sebastian wanted to shout after her, give her a shake—or seduce her all over again.

And there was the rub of it. In mere days, his new wife was provoking him to forget all the rules he had adopted to ensure that his heart and his happiness were never at risk again.

She had to go to Cornwall before he lost the last of his wits.

Indeed, it might be too late for that.

They journeyed in silence the rest of the way to London, stopping only for one night. Sebastian did not come to Eurydice, despite her hopes that he might. He sent Jenkins to summon her in the morning and met her at the carriage. He made the necessary polite motions, but his attention was elsewhere, his expression impassive and his gaze distant.

Sadly, his ill humor was not fading.

Nor was Eurydice's resolve.

How could he fail to explain to her what she had done wrong? Truly, it must be a matter of some intimacy, but they were man and wife. There should be no secrets about their lovemaking. It was only common courtesy to explain to her, but he denied her that.

The argument could not be undone, but worse, Eurydice had no notion how to repair the damage. Each hour they passed in silence together made her more sharply aware of what she had lost. She missed his charm and their conversations. She missed his smile and the mischievous glint that lit his eyes. She missed having his attention and to be sure, she missed his kisses. If this was to be her future, it was a grim prospect.

She liked Sebastian.

No, Eurydice realized in the vicinity of Norwich, she was falling in love with him. She wanted a marriage in every way, a partnership and a union, and in that, she suspected she was a fool. What if the duke was right about his friend's nature? She no longer desired to retreat to Cornwall, for there she would be without Sebastian. The prospect of hours alone, a large library and time to write lost its appeal without regular interactions with her husband.

At the same time, she could not rescind her invitation to the duke, lest Alexander conclude that she was unhappy and challenge Sebastian to a duel. She could not change the invitation, inviting Daphne to visit her alone in Cornwall, for that would scarce convince anyone of her marital bliss. She could not bear to leave Sebastian, yet she could not live with his cold indifference.

If she told him of her growing regard, she did not doubt that he would laugh at her—or claim that he had succeeded in winning her heart after all.

What a wretch he was, challenging her every notion and leaving her feelings in a muddle—when his apparently were not engaged in the least. He had said he had no interest in maidens, and he had lost all interest in her when she had failed abed.

Surely, there had to be books she could consult...

They arrived at his London house without having exchanged more than two words all day. The staff were outside the door to greet her, so Sebastian must have written to announce their arrival and her presence. Sebastian introduced them all to her, with no sign of pleasure, though she thought she detected a gleam of approval in the eye of the butler, Watson. He was an older gentleman and Eurydice hoped he had served the family long enough to know some of her husband's secrets.

It would take some delicacy to encourage his confidence, but Eurydice was determined that it should be done.

She had to make this marriage work.

She had to ensure she gave every appearance of happiness in less than one month's time. Her sister would not be fooled.

And she wanted to regain Sebastian's attention. Somehow, she would seduce him this very night. Perhaps enthusiasm, or the surprise of an invitation to her chamber before the passing of a week, would suffice. Eurydice was desperate.

Sebastian clearly did not share her view. He turned to the driver. "My wife will have need of the coach tomorrow morning, if you please, for she will journey to Rockmorton Manor."

The driver blinked. "In Cornwall, sir?"

"The very same," Sebastian said with a tight smile. "I doubt the house has moved." The driver flushed but Sebastian had already turned to Eurydice. She hated that she was to be dismissed, like a naughty child. "I wish you a good journey," he said to her, his tone formal. "I will absent myself, anticipating that you will leave in the morning."

Eurydice gasped. He could not do this! "But I..."

He fixed her with a steely look. "It was our initial arrangement, my lady. Perhaps I will see you in the spring."

Eurydice could not argue with him, much less correct him, in front of his entire staff—and he knew it.

Sebastian bowed to her, then pivoted and strode into the street, calling for a cab as his own carriage was unpacked before his house. Eurydice watched him go, well aware of the surprise of the household. She did not have to wonder at his destination. He would visit a mistress or courtesan to ensure his satisfaction, and gain the pleasure she had not granted to him.

Miss Esmeralda Ballantyne, no doubt.

Even if he had sent that letter from Airdfinnan, the lady in question would have only just received it and would certainly welcome him back into her affections.

It turned out that Eurydice's original plan was highly unsatisfactory, after all.

Sebastian clearly did not share her doubts, for he did not spare her a backward glance.

Eurydice squared her shoulders, fixing a confident smile on her lips before she turned to face the staff. "He has so missed his club," she said. Leaving no interval for speculation, she confessed to Watson that she had no ladies' maid. "At Airdfinnan, I shared my sister's maid and of course, I could not persuade her to leave with me."

"I shall seek a suitable lady's maid for you at once, my lady," Watson vowed. With a flick of his wrist, the other servants returned to their tasks. A word from the older man and the footmen were bringing in the luggage, Jenkins was directing those who carried Sebastian's portmanteau and arrangements were being made for the horses to return to the stables.

And Eurydice was entering her new home, alone.

❧

The house was graciously proportioned, though not as grand as the duke's London residence, which had been designed for entertaining. Eurydice had not expected Sebastian's house to be as large, and truly, she found its size both cozy and charming. The duke's homes could be somewhat daunting in their splendor: this one reminded her of the dower house at North Barrows where she had passed much of her childhood. It was a home for a family.

The decor was elegant and it was scrupulously clean. The dining room was flooded with sunlight, which she liked, and the library had a considerable stock of books, as well as two promising chairs by the fireplace. There was another pair of doors that seemed to be secured. The house had an air of welcome that Eurydice admired and one that made her wonder about Sebastian's family. She knew vaguely that his parents had passed away, but would have assumed as much since he had come into his inheritance. She also knew that he had no siblings. Her curiosity grew with every step she progressed into the house. There were miniatures in one cabinet, but she did not ask Watson about them as yet.

The butler led her up the stairs to the next floor where there seemed to be four rooms, two facing the street and two facing the back of the house. He led her to one at the back, which was bright with morning sunlight and comfortably furnished. "How lovely. Thank you, Watson."

"I trust it will suit, my lady." The older man turned to leave.

There were beautiful watercolors framed on the wall and Eurydice moved to study them. She was hungry for details about Sebastian's life and family, for he had surrendered little. "Did someone in the family paint these, Watson? They are admirably well done."

"The mother of the current earl, my lady. She often painted *en plein air* at Rockmorton Manor."

Sebastian's parents. He had never spoken of them. Was there a reason? "She was talented."

"Indeed, my lady. A most gracious and talented lady."

Eurydice realized then what she hadn't seen yet in the house. "Is there a portrait of her?"

The butler seemed startled. "In the drawing room, my lady, there is a fine portrait done of the earl and his lady just after the arrival of their son, the current earl."

"I should like very much to see it."

"The drawing room, my lady, has been closed up these twelve years," he began, warning her.

Eurydice smiled. "I would like to see the portrait," she said crisply. "And then I will have a cup of tea in the library." With any luck, she would find a reference to her current conundrum there.

Watson, like the servants in the duke's household, responded well to firm instruction. "Excellent, my lady."

Eurydice removed her hat, coat and gloves, then followed Watson to that pair of doors. They were locked and when he opened them, she saw that he had told no tale. A cloud of dust rose from the floor inside. The furniture looked ghostly, draped in cloths, and the shades were drawn against the daylight. He moved ahead of her, obviously familiar with the room and its contents, and opened a pair of drapes. Dust motes danced in the sunbeam that slanted into the room, and Eurydice saw that it was a graceful room, decorated in apricot and gold. There was a harpsichord in one corner and a large beautifully carved fireplace dominating the opposite wall. An ornate gold clock sat on the mantle, protected by a glass dome.

And over the mantle was hung a very large portrait in a gilt frame.

"Why was this room closed up, Watson? It is lovely."

"It was done after the earl and his wife died, my lady. The current earl wished it so."

She turned to look at him. "When did they pass?"

"Twelve years ago, my lady, on the same day."

She assumed there had been an accident, which was how her parents had come to their end. "The same day?" she echoed, inviting more of the tale.

The butler cleared his throat. "It was most unfortunate, my lady. The earl took ill and when he developed pneumonia, his wife insisted upon nursing him herself. She took the illness after him, and they died within hours of each other."

Eurydice felt her throat tighten at this sad news. "And the present earl?"

"Was here, my lady. His mother had sent him to town lest he take the illness as well. She always feared for his welfare, given that he was their only child." He coughed gently and Eurydice understood he had more to say, if she invited it.

"Did he realize his father was so ill?" she asked,

making a guess.

"He did not, my lady, at his mother's insistence. She wanted him to enjoy Christmas as always they had together, and she believed the former earl would recover." He shook his head. "Alas, she was mistaken." His voice broke just a little and Eurydice understood that this couple had been held in high affection by their staff.

They must have been good people.

Eurydice stopped before the portrait and studied the depicted couple. They were handsome, to be sure, young and clearly happy. The man was tall like Sebastian and there was something in his smile that reminded her of her husband at his most mischievous. He looked down at the lady, who was seated in a chair, one slippered foot extended. She was a glorious beauty, with ebony hair and rosy cheeks, dark eyes glinting with pleasure. The object of her delight was the toddler in her lap, a laughing young boy who had to be Sebastian. The image was so filled with love and joy that Eurydice's throat tightened.

This was what Sebastian had known. He had grown up, surrounded and bolstered by such love, and its loss could only have rent his heart in two. She would have been more devastated if she had been older when her parents died, old enough to have known them well and loved them truly. How fortunate he had been—she could almost envy him—but she recognized that the loss of his parents, both at once, would have been devastating.

That was why he had insisted that the room be closed up.

"Christmas," she said, realizing only now the import of the butler's words.

"Yes, my lady. They passed on December 25."

No wonder Sebastian despised the festive season. Did he blame himself for his parents' death? He certainly might blame himself for not being with them at the end, even though it had been no fault of his own.

He would have the world believe that he did not care, but Eurydice began to understand that, perhaps, he cared too much.

What if she could restore his joy of the festive season? What if she could give him that sense of a secure home that he had to miss? Eurydice had only vague memories of her parents and their love, but she knew very well the rooting that Lady Octavia had given her. She had felt safe at the dower house of North Barrows and secure in the promise of the future.

She had to at least suggest as much to Sebastian before she went to Cornwall.

"Thank you, Watson," she said, hearing the unevenness of her own voice. "It is a glorious portrait."

"Indeed, it is, my lady," he said with a bow. "If you will take your repose in the library, I will bring you tea there."

"Thank you, Watson." She knew she did not imagine that the butler beamed at her before he bowed and departed. She had need of one ally, and it seemed she had found one already.

Perhaps Watson could help.

To Watson's delight, the earl had not just married on whim but had taken a sensible woman to wife. The butler had heard of Miss Eurydice Goodenham, of course, for there had been much chatter about her older sister marrying the Duke of Inverfyre, but he had known very little about the younger sister's nature. Just moments in her presence reassured him enormously as to her character.

And truly, the earl's abrupt departure and his command—one which his wife had no intention of following—proved that this lady had shaken his assumptions. Watson had known the earl from infancy and had thought for some years that a challenge would do him good.

That challenge had arrived in the person of his new wife.

By the time Watson had sent out a call for a lady's maid and carried the tea to the library, the lady was there with a stack of books by her side. To his relief, a fire had been lit in that room and she was seated before it, engrossed in one of them.

She looked up with a smile as he set down the tray. "Thank you, Watson."

He poured her tea, noting that she drank it strong and clear, and to his surprise, she cleared her throat.

"If I might have a word, Watson," she said and he nodded agreement.

"Of course, my lady." At her quick glance, he shut the door to the library and returned to stand before her, waiting.

"It appears I have made a *faux-pas*, but it cannot be undone and I would request your assistance in salvaging the situation."

Watson was intrigued. The lady did not strike him as impulsive or flighty and he could not imagine what error she might have made. "Of course, my lady."

She looked down at her tea, choosing her words. "The earl and I chose to wed hastily, as you must have guessed, and exchanged our vows at Coldstream the day before yesterday. My sister is married to the Duke of Inverfyre and it was from his Scottish home, Airdfinnan, that we departed with the intent to marry." She took a sip of tea. "The duke—" she added with care as she set the cup and saucer aside "—was not pleased." She met Watson's gaze, inviting his understanding.

"I see, my lady."

"He pursued us, with the objective of ensuring my return to Airdfinnan and that of challenging the earl to a duel."

Watson struggled to keep his brows from rising.

"And so, when the duke located us on the morning after our nuptials, I knew that his concern was an echo of my sister's fears for my welfare. I insisted that ours was a match destined for success, but the duke remained skeptical. To see such concerns set at rest, I invited the duke, the duchess, and their two young sons here for Christmas dinner."

"Ah," Watson could only manage to say.

"I had no notion that the earl did not celebrate Christmas or that he routinely granted a day's leave to his staff. He was and is vexed with me for issuing this invitation, but I will not rescind it. The earl must not be compelled to duel with the duke." She spoke firmly. "His honor will insist that he accept the challenge, but he has told me that the duke is a much better shot. They have known each other for a long time."

"Indeed, my lady. We have welcomed the Duke of Inverfyre here on occasion."

She inhaled. "And even my husband insists that the duke will not waste his shot, not when he believes he defends the honor of his wife's family. The rift must be repaired, and I see this invitation as the simplest way of managing that." She appealed to him with a look.

Watson could only agree with her conclusion.

"I understand, my lady." He straightened. "Will the duke and his family be staying here, my lady?"

"I expect they will prefer to stay at the duke's own townhouse in Grosvenor Square. Doubtless my sister will write to accept the invitation and confirm their plans with me. She is very organized." She smiled with obvious affection. "Their boys are darling but quite active. They may leave us turned upside-down in just those few hours."

Watson could not help but smile. "It has been a long time since there were children at Rockmorton House, my lady."

"The earl and I will endeavor to see that changed, Watson," she replied, the implication clear that such a goal could only be pursued if her rift with the earl was also repaired. "I should so appreciate your help with this event. I do not wish to add to my blunder, and in fact, I must find a way to restore my husband's confidence in me."

Watson bowed. "You may leave the preparations to me, my lady. We have had the honor of the Duke of Inverfyre's presence here before, as mentioned, and I will ensure that every preparation is made for his...reassurance."

This time, the lady's smile lit her eyes. She was a very pretty lady. "Thank you, Watson." She paused for a moment, revealing that she knew the import of her next words. "Perhaps the drawing room could be cleaned, the better that we can entertain our guests."

"Of course, my lady." Watson bowed again. "There will be three candidates in the morning for the post of your lady's maid, with the hope that one meets with your satisfaction. On this day, Millicent, the head housemaid, can be of service to you. You need not be concerned about the servants on Christmas Day—most of them miss the bustle of the festivities in a big house."

She nodded, then settled a little deeper into her chair. "I feel very fortunate to have arrived at a house so well in hand. Thank you again, Watson."

Watson bowed and left, feeling rather fortunate in his new mistress himself.

CHAPTER SIX

Sebastian had no notion what to do.

That was a new situation for him and an utterly unwelcome one. He was falling in love with a practical woman who did not believe in love—not only was she his wife, but she wished for a financial settlement. There was a jest in that if he had the will to unearth it, but Sebastian did not.

He did not want to be home.

He did not want to be elsewhere.

He wanted to be with Eurydice, but that would not do, not until he had decided upon a course of action. Had his wife been any other woman, he could have cast himself at her feet, begged forgiveness and charmed her into accepting his love in the blink of an eye. The strategy would scarcely be a success with Eurydice—which was, of course, the heart of her appeal. She defied his every expectation and he adored her.

Sebastian Montgomery was smitten.

Yet if he confessed as much, Eurydice would be disappointed in him for such a show of emotion. Had she not said she could not respect a man driven by his emotions?

He walked along the Serpentine and then Pall Mall, seeking a solution to his woes. How did one persuade a woman like Eurydice to fall in love? He had no notion. She was not seduced by his charm, she was immune to his commands, she challenged his expectations, broke the rules of his household, made him laugh, brightened his days—and could not have cared less about him or his fate, so long as he consulted a solicitor before he died. Never had a woman so confounded him.

Never had he been so enchanted by an amorous union. Not only did the responsibility of introducing Eurydice to pleasure change all for him, but her reactions and her joy had made it a marvelous night. He wanted more. He wanted her every day and every night, he never wanted to be parted from her—she would conceive with haste and laugh at his weakness for her.

Then she would read a book, abandoning him to agony.

He had been a fool to accept her proposal.

Eurydice had not known about the agonizing loss of his parents and could not have known that he blamed himself for accepting his mother's instruction at her word. He had been merrily enjoying himself in town while his father and then his mother fought for their survival—and drunk in the bed of a courtesan when they both died. He had thought he was celebrating the season, as bidden to do.

Instead, he had been so selfish that he had not even realized the two people of greatest importance to him in the world were dying.

For twelve years, he had lived with his guilt, insisting upon solitude so he could never fail anyone else. He had lived supposedly for pleasure alone, but really, he had been evading the responsibility of caring about anything or anyone.

Then came Eurydice into his life. Within days, if not hours, her practical wager had begun to change into something greater. The minx was destroying his barriers and melting the ice in his heart with fearsome speed—and he had realized as much when she had not just invited Armstrong to visit at Christmas, but did so to save Sebastian's hide.

It was no jest that Armstrong would triumph in a duel, but Eurydice's concern had not been indicative of any tender emotion. He had not yet amended his will to include her and ensure her future security.

Practical Eurydice would laugh at him if she knew his emotional state, and then she would tease him for it.

If she did not pity him.

It was a situation beyond his ability to repair. If nothing else, Sebastian could see one detail resolved.

He went to his solicitor and made the modification to his will, leaving his entire estate to Eurydice and any children of their union. He then went to his club and drank a large brandy quickly. It was only late afternoon, he had not eaten and he had not downed a brandy in a long while. The liquor set a fire within him that warmed him in a way that was not unpleasant.

Sebastian called for another and soon lost track of the time.

The morning after their arrival in town, Watson informed Eurydice that the carriage was waiting for her, just as the earl had instructed. Eurydice had enjoyed an excellent breakfast, though she had not slept well.

She had perused the books in the library, working her way through every single shelf, and had found no reference to assist her. There were law tomes and histories, many volumes concerning the natural flora of England, and a considerable collection of books on animal husbandry and farming. She explored every volume of promise but did not find a word of advice on intimate matters between man and wife. There were no less than three books of manners and four on conduct at court, and it was probably a good thing that none of them had chapters about the amorous arts. There was precious little literature to Eurydice's thinking, though she thought it a sad measure of her desperation that she would seek illumination about such a subject from novels.

Sebastian had not returned for dinner so she had eaten alone, then descended to the kitchen to thank the staff. She talked of her plans for Christmas Day with them and knew they did not feign their enthusiasm. Watson vowed that he would recall every detail of how the former lady had seen the festive season celebrated and Eurydice left with a list and a lighter heart.

It would have been better yet if she had encountered her husband.

She had no notion when Sebastian had returned during the night, or even if he had, but no one in the household appeared to be concerned so she did not ask. It seemed that a wife should know if her husband was in residence.

At breakfast, the newspapers from that very day had been delivered—at Airdfinnan, they were typically two or even three days old—but Eurydice found no pleasure in them. As she pulled on her gloves, she suggested to Watson that Millicent would suit her well enough and that he should perhaps hire another house maid. She left the house to meet the carriage.

"Have you no luggage, my lady?" the driver asked.

"Not to visit Brisbane's Emporium," she said with a smile. "If you would be so good as to take me there and wait. I doubt I will be long."

Driver and footman exchanged a significant

glance, but Eurydice did not concern herself with that. "Yes, my lady."

There was one soul in all of London whom Eurydice could ask for advice of a most intimate nature. By wondrous coincidence, Sophie de Roye was also the owner of Brisbane's Emporium, the establishment Eurydice was determined to patronize in the decorating of Rockmorton House for the holidays. There was nothing in the way of decorations, Watson had informed her, and she could only imagine that assistance in the preparation of festive treats would be welcome. She had a list of staff and intended to procure small gifts for each of them, just as Daphne did each year at Airdfinnan. Eurydice was glad of her older sister's example in this, for before Daphne had wed the duke, their lives had been much simpler. With any luck, she would not err and embarrass Sebastian.

The halls of Brisbane's Emporium were decked in Christmas splendor. There were holly and ivy garlands draped behind the counters and mistletoe arrangements dangling overhead, ready to be taken home and installed in one's foyer. A group of men and women with angelic voices were singing carols in the lobby, collecting donations for the poor. A baker had set up a seasonal shop just inside the main entrance, offering sausage rolls, shortbread, plum puddings and mince pies for those who declined to make their own. There was eggnog and mulled wine to take home, and gingerbread that could be enjoyed in the store. An entire counter was laden with brightly colored candy, making it the object of fascination for many children. The counters were filled with glorious gifts—shawls and pins and fans and purses, snuffboxes, pins and tempting trinkets—to acquire for one's loved ones. The aisles were bustling and Eurydice could fairly hear the coins adding up. Just the sight of the festive displays raised her spirits.

They would have a Yule log at Airdfinnan and the boys would be excited by the prospect of gifts. The duke would put his ledgers away early each night to read them tales before the fire, and during the day, there would be long walks or rides. The fires would crackle and Eurydice sighed that she was missing such familiar joys.

But she would make her own joys in her own home.

She wound her way through the shoppers and found Sophia in the very thick of it all, looking both happy and busy. Eurydice knew that her former governess had a daughter and a son now, but Sophia's eyes danced just as merrily as ever and her freckles seemed to have multiplied.

"Eurydice Goodenham!" that woman cried with pleasure and seized her hands, then kissed her cheeks. "How did I not know that you were coming to town? Are you staying at the duke's house? Where is your sister?"

"They are yet in Scotland," Eurydice confessed and Sophia fell silent, her gaze becoming guarded. "I am here alone." She flushed under Sophia's stern eye and continued before she could be chided. "With my new husband," she confessed in a whisper.

Sophia's eyes widened, then she ushered Eurydice into the back room, securing the door against listening ears. "And how did I not know that you were married?" she demanded.

Eurydice surrendered her shopping list first and Sophia dispatched a clerk to see it fulfilled and packed in the carriage. She then ordered tea. Eurydice explained about her elopement and Alexander's fury with the situation, watching her former governess' disapproval grow steadily.

Sophia frowned, then took Eurydice's hands in hers again. Her expression was solemn. "I could write to the duke and the marriage could be annulled..."

"It cannot be annulled."

"Then you are..."

"Yes, and so I must remain here. Sebastian cannot resume his affairs with courtesans and actresses, not until I conceive his child. That is the only way to keep our wager." She bit her lip and Sophia squeezed her hands.

"Do you love him, Eurydice?"

Eurydice shook her head. "I thought not. I thought it impossible, but...now I wonder."

"And does he love you?"

"I fear he was disappointed by another."

Sophia was dismissive. "Yet she is gone and you are his wife. You must work with the opportunity presented, Eurydice."

"But I fear that the true issue is not my invitation to the duke, but Sebastian's own disappointment in the match."

Sophia was outraged. "Why should he be disappointed in you? You are clever and..."

"Decidedly inexperienced abed."

"That is an asset in a lady, Eurydice. Never forget as much. He cannot have expected otherwise."

"But he may have wished for more. In fact, I am certain he must have done. And now he dreads the ordeal of a regular seduction. Worse, I cannot find a reference to assist me."

"A reference?"

"A book. All knowledge is in books."

Sophia laughed as if she knew she should not. "Oh, Eurydice, all knowledge is not in books, especially that of the most intimate kind."

"Then how will I learn?"

"You must learn to seduce your husband yourself," her former governess said in a tone that brooked no opposition. "Give him your undivided attention. Ask him about his interests. Truly, Eurydice, you are good at conversation and better at winning approval than you appreciate. Talk to the man..."

But Eurydice could not do as much if Sebastian did not return home.

Had he gone to a lover?

Or had some dire fate befallen him?

And how could she possibly learn to seduce him without guidance.

She put down her tea when she realized that one person in London might possess the answers to all those questions, and more. But did she dare to call on Esmeralda Ballantyne?

Esmeralda Ballantyne had seen a great deal of the world and its marvels, not to mention a hearty measure of human foible, but she had never seen Sebastian Montgomery in his cups. She fairly tripped over him in a gaming hell, astonished because she had not realized he had returned to town.

Her first thought was that he was pretending to be more drunk than he was, then she saw how badly he was losing. She had never seen him lose, either. What was wrong with him? In a rare protective urge, she interrupted the game, scooped Sebastian up with the assistance of several servants, and took him home.

He slept all that night and would not leave his chamber the next day.

"You are brooding," she charged when he would not unlock the door. She rattled the knob, to no avail, even though this was her house.

"I am thinking," he muttered, his voice low and gravely.

It was on the tip of her tongue to advise him not to injure himself with the uncustomary activity, but she knew it was a waspish comment—and one borne of her own awareness of his disinterest in her. "Am I not to be thanked for my intervention?" she asked. "You might have lost a fortune last night." There was no reply but she heard a rustle of paper. She saw a note being slipped beneath the door and frowned with impatience even as she picked it up.

It was addressed to her.

It was dated some days ago and advised her of Sebastian's marriage.

"Who on earth is Miss Eurydice Goodenham?" she asked, not truly expecting a reply. The door had been somewhat taciturn thus far.

"My wife," he growled. "Leave me be, please, Esmeralda."

Esmeralda frowned. "Do you love her?"

"I promised my fidelity to her until she bears our son and my heir."

Esmeralda read the note again. "Then you do love her," she said softly, knowing full well that the Earl of Rockmorton would not have made such a concession otherwise. "What are you doing here?" she demanded, less softly than she had spoken before. "Should you not be with your wife?" She bit off the last word just as Sebastian opened the door. He looked rumpled, dangerous and utterly seductive.

"She does not believe in love," he said.

"Then you should change her mind," Esmeralda replied.

"I cannot..."

"You changed mine," she admitted, the edge of disappointment in her voice.

He looked so astounded that she knew he had never guessed. "But..."

Esmeralda turned away. "Go home, Sebastian."

"She is not romantic. She is practical," he said as Esmeralda walked to the summit of the stairs. "I do not know how to proceed and I fear..." He frowned and shook his head, falling silent.

"You fear?" she prompted by this hint that he cared about anything at all.

"To lose her, of course. To go through that pain again."

She had never guessed that he had endured a loss. In all their time together and supposed intimacy, he had never shared that. He had shared his body but no more, while she had been prepared to surrender everything. All for nothing. What manner of bargain was that? Worse yet, he had not known. He had thought their transaction fair.

Impatience rose hot within Esmeralda and made her speak when she should have remained silent. "Then you are a witless fool and you will lose her. That will do your heart more injury, for the situation will be entirely your own fault."

Esmeralda descended the stairs and had just poured herself a small glass of wine when her butler cleared his throat. "A lady to see you."

She glanced toward him and he inclined his head, offering the card.

Miss Eurydice Goodenham.

She stared at the card as if it was written in Sanskrit. Respectable women did not come to Esmeralda's house—in fact, many respectable men avoided it. The wives of men Esmeralda entertained most certainly did not call upon her.

Did Sebastian's new wife know that he was in her guest bedroom?

How could she know?

What else could she possibly want?

There were those who would have found it amusing that Esmeralda was to play matchmaker for the first time in all her days, but she was not one of them. Her heart was breaking even as she indicated that the lady should be shown in.

❧

Miss Ballantyne's house had not been difficult to find. It was small and a bit tawdry in Eurydice's view, but she expected the choice of colors would look their best at night. There was a lot of gold and a substantial amount of purple, as well as feathers and velvet beyond expectation. She had no doubt that she was not amongst the lady's typical callers.

She was received, which was a relief, and shown into a drawing room of unusually lush reds and pinks. In the midst was Esmeralda herself, her dark sleek hair perfectly done, her pale silk dress revealing as much of her figure as it covered, and the emeralds in her lavish necklace matching her eyes perfectly. She seemed to be faintly amused, and her gaze flicked over Eurydice in a way that made

Eurydice keenly aware of the differences between them.

"I understand that you have some acquaintance with my husband, Sebastian Montgomery, the Earl of Rockmorton," she began when her hostess did not speak.

"I am and I do," the lady acknowledged. "Will you take tea?"

"Thank you." Eurydice accepted the cup of tea she did not want and tried to summon her audacity. "I know this is unconventional, but I hope that you will grant me a favor."

Esmeralda smiled. "You may have heard that I have little interest in convention," she said, pouring herself a cup of tea. She remained standing, as did Eurydice, but sipped her tea as she waited.

"I know little of men and their satisfaction," Eurydice admitted, her cheeks burning. "But I would like to ensure that my husband finds pleasure in our union. Could you teach me something of the arts of seduction?"

Her hostess choked on her tea in that very moment. She put it down, the cup clattering in the saucer. "You wish to learn the arts of seduction?" she echoed.

Eurydice nodded. "Solely to be a good wife and partner to my husband, of course," she added, feeling her face become yet more red. "I know that he has expectations and I fear that I have not fulfilled them adequately as yet. All skills can be learned, with diligence and practice, however I have been unable to find a suitable reference. That is why I am asking you. You know more of him in such matters of intimacy, after all." Her speech completed, she took a breath and fixed her hopeful gaze upon Esmeralda.

Her hostess stared down at her cup. "Forgive my surprise. I have never been asked such a question," she admitted.

At her gesture, Eurydice sat down, perching on the lip of a settee best intended for lounging. She surveyed her surroundings again, feeling the worst was behind her. She had asked: the reply was out of her hands. "This is quite a remarkable room."

"Do you think so?"

"I do. It is more feminine than any drawing room I have visited before, more like a lady's bedchamber." She smiled at her hostess. "I like all the roses, and the pink hues suit you well. You look like another flower in their midst."

The lady again seemed to be without words. She sipped her tea as did her guest.

"I profess myself surprised that you have never been asked such a question," she said. "For one consults experts in all other matters. How does one learn these skills then?"

Her hostess's eyes widened slightly. "I believe husbands often tutor their wives."

"Is that how you learned the amorous arts?"

"I have never wed," the lady confessed. "I have never felt the compulsion."

"I can well understand that impulse. I would not

have done as much myself if it had not been a question of financial security. And now, I must keep my side of the bargain."

"I see." Her hostess frowned. "Perhaps you should ask your husband."

"Well, that is the trouble," Eurydice confessed. Miss Ballantyne was remarkably easy to talk to. "He is not speaking to me and I am not entirely certain of his whereabouts." She sipped her tea. "I have vexed him mightily, I fear."

Miss Ballantyne's eyes began to sparkle. "Perhaps that is good for him," she whispered.

"I do not understand."

"It is not healthy for anyone to have all matters proceed their way." Miss Ballantyne seemed to have made a decision for she set her cup aside and rose smoothly to her feet. "I predict that he will return shortly and suggest that you ask him for this advice."

"About the amorous arts?"

Miss Ballantyne nodded and smiled. "He might quite enjoy the tutelage." She crossed the room and lifted a small book from a shelf, eying it for a moment before pivoting and presenting it to Eurydice. "And in the meantime, this might give you some of the answers you seek."

"Thank you!" Eurydice did not even have time to read the title before she heard a footfall on the stairs.

"Eurydice?" Sebastian demanded from the doorway. "I thought I heard your voice." He looked as far from his usual composed self as was possible. Indeed, he looked tired and more than a little haggard. His cravat was undone and he was not wearing a jacket at all.

He looked like a man who had just risen from bed. At this hour of the afternoon, Eurydice could guess what he had been doing there. Had he not been the one to recommend lovemaking at this very time of day? She straightened, knowing her color was high.

"What are you doing here?" he asked.

"I could ask you the same, sir."

"But you were going to Cornwall."

"No, you instructed me to go to Cornwall, but I did not obey, sir. I had no intention of going, not with my sister coming for Christmas." Eurydice glared at him, so disappointed that she wanted to weep. "I had thought to secure the future of our marriage instead, but I see the fullness of my error now. You need not fear for my obedience: I will now leave you to your leisure of choice." With that, she curtsied to her hostess—who looked decidedly amused—then pivoted and left the house, her chin held high. Sebastian called after her, he even swore mightily, but Eurydice was not swayed.

How *dare* he?

And how could she have been so wrong about him?

He was precisely the rogue she had believed him to be at first, and she had been fool enough to fall in love with him.

Alexander had been right.

In his absence, Sebastian's house had been transformed. He stood in the foyer for a long moment, fighting the colossal headache that was the reward for his sins, and wondered if he had entered the wrong house. Although it was not completed, the foyer was adorned with greenery and red ribbons on one side, a festive display that his mother might have contrived. Greenery and more ribbons were being woven around the bannister and he could smell beeswax candles burning. The doors to the drawing room were open instead of securely locked, and four maids were busily cleaning it. He could smell fresh baking from the kitchen and heard the laughter of busy maids. The house was warm and fairly glowing, so welcoming that he might have been transported thirteen years into the past.

Watson, however, glowered at him with a new level of disapproval from the base of the stairs. This was unassailably his house.

Sebastian approached the drawing room doors warily, as if the illusion might be shattered by proximity, then looked upon the room that he had not seen in years. It was an attractive room, but his gaze rose immediately to the large portrait over the mantle and his throat tightened. "Why is this room opened?" he asked, knowing that Watson had followed him.

"Because your lady wife instructed that it should

be, sir."

"But I have instructed otherwise."

"It had to be prepared when we understood that the Duke of Inverfyre and his family would be arriving for Christmas dinner." Watson's lips tightened. "While the duke has been at ease in the library on previous occasions, his family cannot be accommodated in such a confined space." The older man sniffed. "If you would prefer that it be closed up again, my lord, now that there is no prospect of guests, I will ensure that is done."

Sebastian gave his butler a wary look. "My wife has rescinded her invitation then?"

"Lady Rockmorton has declared she will not be in residence for Christmas." This clearly was the root of the older man's sour mood. Sebastian supposed that he had liked Eurydice, which was only reasonable.

He liked Eurydice himself.

Would he have a chance to tell her of his love? His ears still burned from Esmeralda's challenge and her amusement at his predicament. He had not been able to get a cab and feared he had arrived too late.

"She cannot have left," he argued, keeping his tone reasonable with an effort.

The butler straightened, his expression formidable. "I believe she was bidden to do so," he said, his tone frosty with disapproval.

Sebastian charged up the stairs and knocked upon the door of the chamber Eurydice must have used. It was the larger of the two guest chambers. A woman's voice acknowledged his knock and his heart leapt—but when he opened the door, he found only a maid cleaning the fireplace.

Eurydice's belongings were gone. Indeed, the room was so tidy that she might never have been there. He spun and opened the other guest room door, his own chamber, his mother's chamber, and found no sign of his confounding bride.

Of course not. She would be in the library. He leapt down the stairs and flung open that door, only to find Eurydice seated by the fire. She was reading a small book bound in crimson leather. Her bags were packed and set beside her, with her books and umbrella, too. She was wearing her hat and her cloak, though it was unfastened. She looked as if she had been compelled to halt her departure by the siren's call of a particularly compelling volume.

He had been saved by the book.

She eyed him, as fierce as a wet kitten, then glanced down at the volume in question and continued to read.

"I must apologize," Sebastian said, closing the door behind himself, both to ensure that she did not flee and to keep the servants from hearing him beg her forgiveness.

"With what expectation?" she demanded, dropping the book into her lap. "That I will forgive you for returning to the bed of your mistress, after one—" she held up a finger and shook it at him. He saw only that she had already donned her gloves "—*one* night of coupling that did not meet your expectations?"

She thought him disappointed in their wedding night?

Eurydice did not grant him a chance to reply but swept to her feet, her eyes flashing with fury. "To think that I was fool enough to imagine you a romantic, to hope that we might make a true union in time, that you could even come to love me as I was fool enough to begin to love you. You are a wretch and a cur, a rogue and a scoundrel of the full magnitude of my original expectation, and you are unchivalrous, sir, to grant me what I first requested of you, if only to show how much it is lacking." To his astonishment, tears shone in her eyes and threatened to spill. "You could have left me in my ignorance, sir. You could have never tempted me to care for you, if this had been your intention all along. I knew you to care only for your own whim, but I did not think you *cruel*."

She seized the ties of her cloak but Sebastian heard only one part of her lecture. He touched her arm and she froze, her gaze fixed stubbornly on the floor. He saw the flash of a falling tear and it shattered him utterly, ensuring that he spoke the truth in his heart. "I left, Eurydice, because I could not believe you would ever come to love me as I already love you," he admitted and she looked up, her expression one of wonder. He smiled at her. "I feared not only your mockery but that you would leave me in disappointment."

"Do not tease me, Sebastian," she threatened

huskily. "I could not bear it, not after this day."

"It is the truth, my lady." He took her hand in his, vastly encouraged by her reaction. "If you will consent to be my lady, in every possible way."

"Sebastian!" she whispered, then flung herself at him, dampening his shirt with her tears. They were tears of joy but Sebastian still did not care for them. He kissed her gently and wiped them away, then kissed her with all the passion dawning in his heart. She kissed him back, so sweet and giving that he knew himself to be the most fortunate man in the world.

"The book is right," she whispered when she could speak again. Sebastian did not wish to let her go and kept his arms locked around her as he stared down into her shining eyes.

"What book?"

"The one Miss Ballantyne gave me." She indicated the red volume she had been reading. "*A letter of Genteel and Moral Advice to a Young Lady* by Wetenhall Wilkes. It says 'Never fix your liking on any man that has not those qualities which you have labored after yourself, and who is not likely to be a friend to virtue.'"

"This does not sound like an endorsement of my own nature," Sebastian ventured.

Eurydice laughed. "What you would have people believe of you is not your truth, sir. You are a romantic and you are honorable. You are gallant and kind." Her lashes swept down as her smile turned mysterious in a most delightful way. "And I have no complaint of any of that."

"And here I thought you had found the guide you sought," he said.

She smiled up at him. "Sophia bade me ask you to teach me," she confessed, blushing deeply. "As did Miss Ballantyne."

"But do you intend to tutor me in what you like best, my bold wife?" he teased, delighted to hear her laugh.

"Perhaps we should tutor each other," she suggested, eyes dancing.

"And achieve our goals together: first an heir, then a book."

"If not more of each," she agreed, her happiness more than clear.

Sebastian stole a satisfying kiss. "Then let us lock the door, lady mine, and commence our lessons immediately."

"A fine suggestion, sir," she agreed, then reached to capture his lips with her own. He carried her to the settee before the fire and no one said much of anything for a goodly time.

The cook remarked that night on the vigor of the new couple's appetite for dinner, but Watson only smiled, more satisfied with the situation at Rockmorton House than he had been in years.

EPILOGUE

The weather in December was beastly, to Daphne's thinking. A frigid wind chased the pair of carriages on their southward path from Airdfinnan, stealing every crumb of heat and rocking the vehicles on their path. Sleet fell on the roof and turned the roads to ice, then snow tumbled from the leaden skies in earnest. Worse, Daphne felt dreadful, her innards in such turmoil that she was in peril of being sick in the coach.

Alexander was solicitous and watchful, but she dared not confide her suspicions to him just yet. They stopped at York, then at Thornedyke Manor where his sister, Anthea, and her husband, the baron and Alexander's friend, offered every possible comfort. It was revealed that the couple had decided to journey to London with them, equally curious to witness Eurydice's happiness, and Daphne was glad of Anthea's company.

Malcolm, of course, found it all a grand adventure, no less that he would have additional playmates in Anthea and Rupert's twins. Truth be told, Daphne felt a bit of sympathy for the servants compelled to share the smaller carriage with her sons. On the other hand, it was delightful to have Alexander pull her into his lap and to slumber against his shoulder as the carriage rocked on its seemingly endless journey south.

It took them six more days to reach London, the most trying journey of Daphne's experience. There was snow on the ground when they reached the house in Grosvenor Square, but Findlay was on the steps to greet them and Daphne smiled, certain that all in the house was in readiness.

Alexander scooped her into his arms when she almost slipped and chided her as he carried her to the house. "We should not have made this journey," he said sternly. "You are not well and I will blame myself forever if you take a cold..."

"I do not have a cold, sir, nor am I like to get one with you to warm me."

His blue eyes narrowed as he looked down at her, as fierce as a guardian angel, and she knew she would never cease to be thrilled in his company. "You are not well and do not insist otherwise."

"The carriage rocks so," she confessed. "It was the rhythm that troubled me."

"The carriage is in perfectly good repair," he retorted. "It does not rock any more than customary, even in that ferocious wind. And it never bothers you, at least it has not since—" He stopped on the stairs and looked down at her in shock.

Daphne smiled. "Precisely," she said, smoothing his cravat.

"Again?"

"Again."

Alexander looked so adorably astonished, as if he could not fathom how she might have conceived another child. In truth, the astonishing fact was that they did not yet have a dozen children.

"But you did not tell me," he whispered.

"I did not know for certain. I still do not."

"But..."

"I am no physician, sir."

"But you should have called for one, and then we would have known."

"And then you would have forbidden me to come to London."

His eyes narrowed, though he could not fully hide his pleasure. "You *knew* and you risked your own health."

"I suspected," Daphne corrected. "And I said nothing because I had no choice but to come."

"There is every choice," Alexander began as he carried her up the stairs to her chamber. "We could have come in the summer..."

Daphne silenced him with a fingertip and his gaze dropped to meet hers. "Almost twenty years ago, my sister became my responsibility, Alexander. Though our grandmother subsequently took us in, I had vowed to Eurydice that I would do whatever was necessary to ensure both her welfare and her happiness. Time has not eroded that duty, and indeed, my grandmother reminded me of it when last we spoke." She wriggled and he set her on her feet, still holding fast to her elbow as she wavered. Her tone was fierce, though. "I must be certain that Eurydice is well and that Sebastian will make her a good husband. I do not believe it to be possible, Alexander, and I must be *certain*."

"You should have told me," he said, urging her to a chaise.

She sank into it with gratitude, for it did not rock. "I will tell you whatever tidings I have, when I know them to be true." She leaned back. "But this way, we are here, I can witness the situation myself, and there is a chance that Lady Octavia will not be haunting me over my failed duties."

"There are no ghosts," he chided.

"And you call yourself a Scotsman," she chided in return and he smiled. "Perhaps there might be a cup of beef broth," she said, giving the duke a task so he did not berate her further.

"I shall see to it," he said, brisk and efficient, turning to stride across the chamber. Daphne watched him go, the admiration she felt of both his figure and his nature making her heart glow. It was no mystery why she could not resist him.

"Perhaps a girl this time," she called after him and he glanced back from the doorway.

His gaze warmed at the possibility. "A girl," he

whispered then shook his head, marveling. "Girl or boy will be most welcome, so long as my wife is hale." His voice turned husky. "How can you bring me more joy than already you have, Daphne?"

"I would not wish you to become bored, sir," she teased, drawing off her gloves.

"Never that!" he vowed with a laugh then returned to give her a most satisfying kiss.

One more day and Daphne would know for certain. She could not imagine her sister with that charming rogue, Sebastian Montgomery. As much as she enjoyed his wit and company, he had often vowed he would never wed and she feared for Eurydice's future. She only hoped that all was well.

On the morrow, she would know.

The duke's party arrived at Rockmorton House just after noon, as bidden, while the church bells pealed merrily to herald Christmas Day. Anthea and Rupert were descending from their carriage, and they exchanged joyous greetings in the street. Mme. and M. de Roye rose to greet them in the drawing room, as did Eurydice and Montgomery. The de Roye's daughter, Louisa, was the oldest of the children and immediately began to issue instructions to the younger boys, to noisy result. The children were spirited away to the old nursery by the three nursemaids who had accompanied their charges to London. Alexander smiled that Watson vowed to ensure that the three maids would have a proper tea and he doubted it would take long for the children to fall asleep after the excitements of the day thus far.

Alexander himself was struck by the change in Montgomery's home. He had visited many times over the years and had even stayed in the house, but he had never seen it so filled with life and laughter. It wasn't just decorated for the festive season, something he was certain he had never witnessed, but the drawing room doors that were always closed had been thrown open. The house fairly glowed. The magnificent portrait of Montgomery's happy parents seemed to beam down on the noisy gathering of friends with approval.

The change was remarkable and Alexander could not find fault with it.

He also could not mistake the sparkle in Eurydice's eyes. His wife's younger sister was abundantly happy, it was clear, and Montgomery himself could not seem to keep himself from grinning. Greetings and small gifts were exchanged all around. They had tea and sherry and quite good shortbread, and the children raced through the room at intervals. Lucien, M. de Roye, was encouraged to play the harpsichord, which Alexander suspected had been tuned and pampered precisely for that happy office.

Daphne took her sister aside for a short chat and he was glad to see the sisters laughing together. When his wife returned to his side, she granted him a glance that told him she was satisfied and he was glad of it. The conversation flowed readily, as if all of them had been friends for years, and dinner was a most merry affair.

The clock in the foyer was striking midnight when they rose to return home. There were carolers in the street, their angelic voices carrying through the crisp night air. The guests donned their cloaks and gloves, exchanging farewells and good wishes, then Alexander saw Daphne stare into the shadows beneath the staircase and frown slightly. He followed her gaze and felt this own eyes narrow.

He thought a shadowy figure lingered there, a woman dressed completely in black, her clothing a little old-fashioned and her white hair drawn tightly back. He was startled to realize that he knew only one woman of such appearance but Lady Octavia, once Viscountess of North Barrows, was dead. All the same, the apparition nodded at Daphne and seemed to smile. Alexander heard the faintest of whispers, which might have been the words 'well done,' then he blinked and the vision was gone.

There was just an umbrella stand there, holding one black umbrella with a carved handle. It was an umbrella Alexander remembered well, the one he had heard rapped upon the floor countless times, the one that Eurydice had inherited from her grandmother. He offered his hand to his wife who flushed and smiled, her relief so evident that he did not have to ask after it. He kissed her hand and placed it on his arm to escort her to the carriage, well content with the match he himself had made.

Another child. Could he bear such happiness?

As they crossed the threshold, Alexander heard the decisive rap of an umbrella on the tile floor behind him, but surely that was only his imagination at work.

ABOUT THE AUTHOR

Deborah Cooke sold her first book in 1992, a medieval romance called **Romance of the Rose** published under her pseudonym Claire Delacroix. Since then, she has published over fifty novels in a wide variety of sub-genres, including historical romance, contemporary romance, and paranormal romance. She has published under the names Claire Delacroix, Claire Cross and Deborah Cooke. **The Beauty**, part of her successful Bride Quest series of historical romances, was her first title to land on the *New York Times* List of Bestselling Books. Her books routinely appear on other bestseller lists and have won numerous awards. In 2009, she was the writer-in-residence at the Toronto Public Library, the first time the library has hosted a residency focused on the romance genre. In 2012, she was honored to receive the Romance Writers of America's Mentor of the Year Award.

Currently, she writes historical romances as Claire Delacroix. She also writes paranormal romances and contemporary romances under the name Deborah Cooke. Deborah lives in Canada with her husband and family, as well as far too many unfinished knitting projects.

To learn more about her books, visit her websites:
http://delacroix.net
http://deborahcooke.com